DIRTY MARTINI

A J.J. Graves Mystery

LILIANA HART

ACKNOWLEDGMENTS

A huge thanks to the team of people who help get every book on the shelves!

To my editors—Imogen Howson and Ava Hodge for making me better.

To my cover designer—Dar Albert for always blowing me away with your talent.

To my children—thank you for being amazing! And for getting older. It's fun to run plot ideas by you and have creative responses come back.

To Scott—you're quite simply the best! I love the life we've been blessed with, and I love we get to spend it together.

To my readers—thank you for loving J.J. Graves and sticking with it for eleven books! I've got a lot of stories left to tell.

Any mistakes are mine alone.

Kaal Dracarian. He had to truly *become* Kaal Dracarian. He closed his eyes and exhaled, putting himself back in his battle preparations.

The last piece was intricately made—an heirloom sewn painstakingly by his wife before she'd been slaughtered by the Keoghs—and he touched the silver velvet between his thumb and forefinger, bringing his love's image to mind.

In reality, it had been his mother that had sewn his outer garment and given it to him for his birthday, but that didn't have the same pizazz as the story he'd made up about his nonexistent wife. He'd even found a picture on the internet of what he imagined her to look like and printed out her picture to tape to the wall in his dorm room. Her name was Vida, may she rest in peace.

He brought his fingers to his lips and kissed them, and then pulled on the outer garment. It was trimmed with burgundy and silver thread, and it fit snugly around his torso with all the armor beneath. In lieu of sleeves there were metal shoulder plates, matching the metal studs that completed the intricate design of the outer garment. Flowing to his waist was a cape that hung from one shoulder, the back side the shimmering silver with his family crest and the inside burgundy.

Kevin looked at the clock again, and a rivulet of sweat snaked down his temple and to the corner of his eye, causing his makeup to run. He blinked rapidly and then grabbed his leather fingerless gloves and pulled them on. And then he reached to the nape of his neck and unfurled the chain mail hood, bringing it up over his head. It was the *pièce de résistance*. His crowning glory. It's what made him Kaal Dracarian.

He flexed his fingers and then picked up the two battle-axes that were propped against the wall. They'd been modified. He'd wanted to use authentic axes, but he hadn't been able to lift them. He'd used almost three years of birthday money on replacing the axe-heads with a lightweight steel. The unfortunate thing was that he had to keep the blade covers on per tournament rules.

Not that he was worried about losing. It was only the first round of the tournament, and he'd drawn Lord Uridak—the evil elvish leader of the Sheol Realm—and though his energy sword was powerful, it was no match for his axes.

Energy crackled from every pore in his being, and he beat his fist against his chest, giving a manly grunt. Then he opened the door of the dressing room and the sound of thousands of fans washed over him.

He ignored the people in the wings in modern clothes with clipboards and headsets, and he headed down the tunnel with a single-minded focus that would make him a champion and the hero of his people.

"Ladies and gentlemen!" the MC said in a booming voice from the center of the ring. "Welcome to the Arena! This is the final fight in round one of the Masters of the Realm. Remember, every

CHAPTER ONE

FLURRIES OF SNOW DANCED ACROSS THE HORIZON, teasing of something more substantial to come. The air was crisp and the sky was a shade of blue that was painful to the eyes when combined with the snow. It would have been a glorious day without the dead body.

I pushed my sunglasses up my nose, and wished I'd waited until summer to get my hair cut so I had some protection on the back of my neck and ears. Of course, I could have remembered my scarf and hat, but that would've been too easy.

My name is J.J. Graves and I was no stranger to doing things the hard way, though I liked to think I'd gotten wiser over the past few years. Apparently, today was not one of those days. But on the bright side, I was having a good hair day, the holidays were over, Jack had just been reconfirmed as sheriff, and having my collar flipped up made me look like a TV detective.

"Nothing makes you feel more ancient than being back on a college campus," I said, matching my stride with Jack's. "Look at these kids all smug and arrogant in their hoodies and weird capes. Why are they wearing capes? Have things changed that much since we were that age?"

Jack snorted out a laugh. "Slow down, Grandma Moses. Though I have to admit I'm confused about the capes too. I feel strangely underdressed."

"I'm always a fan of you being underdressed," I said cheekily.

"Settle down, woman," Jack said. "If you keep undressing me I'm going to have to take out worker's comp. I'm only a man."

"As the person on the receiving end of what happens when you're underdressed, I don't think that's true. I'm not sure you're human. But I'll give you a reprieve until tonight so you can refuel."

"I'm grateful," he said, looking at me wryly.

I took a few seconds to get my fill of him. He was dressed in his normal uniform of jeans and boots, and he wore a khaki button-down shirt with the sheriff's office logo over the breast pocket. The shirt was untucked and he wore a shoulder holster under a brown suede shearling jacket. His badge was clipped to his belt.

He was a work of art to look at—dark hair cut close to the scalp, a few days' worth of beard, bedroom eyes that smoldered when he looked at me, and a scar over his eyebrow that kept him from being too perfect—and there were still moments I weight and blade. "It's lighter than it looks," he said. "The blade is covered."

"Arena Wars rules," Slack said. "Sword tips and axe edges must have a protective covering so no one gets hurt."

"Huh," Jack said, putting down the axe and walking to the far side of the ring to examine the sword that had allegedly killed the boy in front of me.

"Jack," I warned. "Maybe you should get someone to check it out before anyone touches it. You don't know what you're dealing with."

"If this thing becomes an electrical sword that actually works and isn't just a movie prop, I can only think of one person who's brilliant enough to run logistics on the spot, and he's a long way from here."

"Yeah," I said. "Carver is going to be so mad you didn't call him. This is right up his nerd alley."

"Oh, I'm definitely going to call him," Jack said. "We've got new weapons technology that killed someone. We're going to need help on this one. This is some seriously advanced stuff. And it's got to be taken into evidence. I'd rather me do it than one of my guys. Besides, I've got a doctor on-site if things go wrong."

I blew out a sigh. It wasn't easy being married to a hero. They were always doing hero stuff.

Jack knelt by the sword and then looked at Slack. "What can you tell me about Dwight Parr?"

Slack shifted his weight and rested his elbow on

his weapon at his side. "First impression was that he fit right into this kind of scene. He was a mess when I restrained him and put him in the athletic director's office. He couldn't get a coherent word out, and I had to call the EMTs over because he was puffing on that inhaler so much I thought he was going to pass out. They gave him oxygen and calmed him down.

"Even then I couldn't get him to string two words together. I finally got his name from the tournament roster and then looked him up in the KGU database. He's a senior in the honors engineering program. No marks on his school record, no arrest record, and he's got a 4.0. He was recently awarded the Archimedes Fellowship, which is some prestigious grant and acceptance to a program at Oxford over the summer."

"Sounds like Dwight was too smart for his own good," Jack said. He reached for the hilt of the sword and said, "Here goes nothing." And then he wrapped his hand around the hilt.

CHAPTER TWO

I HELD MY BREATH UNTIL I WAS SURE JACK WAS OKAY, and then I exhaled slowly. Technology and engineering weren't my thing. If it was more complicated than my phone, I had a tendency to stay away from it. I could dissect bodies all day long, but if there was a problem with my computer, my eyes glazed over and my brain fried.

"Well," I said once the fear in my chest had subsided. "Now that I'm not going to get to collect your life insurance and logic has prevailed, I guess it makes sense that if Parr struck the blow that sent the current through the victim, then the hilt would be safe enough to keep Parr from falling to the same fate."

Jack nodded. "My thoughts exactly. But it also makes me wonder why Parr would touch the victim, knowing the amount of electricity running through his sword."

"So maybe he didn't know," I said, leaning over

the victim to get a closer look. "He's a student. Maybe he didn't realize the power he'd packed in the volts. Could've been an accident."

"Are enhancements to the weapons allowed?" Jack asked.

"You'd have to ask the coordinator a question like that," Slack said. "She knows all the rules."

"Who's the coordinator?" Jack asked.

"Her name is Trish Johnson," Slack said. "She's around here somewhere with the president of the university and the legal team. They've got some damage control to do. News has already hit the airwaves."

Jack nodded and then came over to where I was kneeling. "What more do you need to do here?"

"I can't do more than a visual here without damaging tissue or compromising evidence," I told him. "The metal from his chain mail is melted to his skin in places. I'm going to have to work some magic to remove it."

"That sounds horrible," Jack said.

"Most likely," I told him. "Fortunately, he won't feel a thing."

Jack rolled his eyes and got back to his feet and then he held out a hand to help me up. "You have an evidence bag on you big enough for this sword?" Jack asked.

"Not even close," I told him.

"There's some trash bags in the supply closet," Slack said, whistling at one of his campus policemen to bring him what he needed.

"Perfect," Jack said. "I appreciate it."

"Sheldon and the new intern should be here any second to remove the body and get him back to the funeral home," I said.

"When did you get a new intern?" Jack asked.

"Today," I said. "I got an email this morning from the University of Virginia telling me they were sending me a new intern. I put in the request weeks ago. I miss Lily already."

"We just saw her three days ago," Jack said.

"I know, but that was in a weird social setting. I'm not sure how I feel about seeing her and Cole together as a couple. She's got stars in her eyes and he looks like he has no idea what he's doing with her. Cole is used to experienced women who are used to the kind of games he plays. He's going to end up breaking her heart and then I'm going to have to kill him."

Jack sighed and his mouth tightened in a straight line. "They're both adults."

"Yeah, well, that's up for debate," I said. "Who knows? Maybe he'll surprise us all and decide to settle down."

Jack grunted and then nodded toward the tunnel. "There's your boy."

I turned and saw Sheldon Durkus wheeling a gurney toward us. The last rays of sunlight shone from the opposite end of the tunnel, giving Sheldon a silhouette that made him look like a small boy dressed in his dad's baggy work clothes.

Sheldon was an unkempt, short man on the

doughy side with a comb-over and Coke-bottle glasses. He was in his mid-twenties and had recently graduated from mortuary school, and I was almost positive he'd be living with his mother the rest of his life. He was brilliant at embalmings, but not so great with living people. There was an innocence about Sheldon that made him endearing, and a golden retriever kind of enthusiasm that made time spent with him best in small doses. Add those qualities to the fact that he was a constant spout of useless information, I'd found that Sheldon made me want to hug him and take up drinking in equal measure.

Behind Sheldon was my new intern. I'd had about ten minutes to talk with him before I'd been called to the crime scene, and I was still undecided on Blake Steed. I'd had to check his paperwork twice to make sure that was his real name. He looked like a young Brad Pitt in *Legends of the Fall*, and with a name like Blake Steed I wondered how he'd ended up in forensic pathology instead of the porn industry. But I guess we could be grateful for small favors.

"That's the new intern?" Jack asked, looking at me and raising his brows.

"That's what they tell me," I said. "Wait until you hear his name."

"Where are you getting your interns from?" Jack asked. "A casting agency?"

"It's starting to feel that way," I said. "I thought Lily was an anomaly, but maybe U of V has a pathology school for beautiful people. I'm not sure it matters. I don't know if it's going to work out with the new guy."

"Why?" Jack asked, surprised. "I thought you needed someone."

"I do," I said. "But if he doesn't stop hitting on me, he's going to end up on my embalming table."

"Who wouldn't want to hit on you with that kind of sweet talk."

I laughed out loud and watched as Sheldon and Blake collapsed the gurney so they could lift it up the stairs and into the ring. Sweat dotted Sheldon's hairless upper lip and he turned an odd shade of green. He dropped his end of the gurney and pulled his shirt over his nose, his hot breath making his glasses fog up.

"Breathe slow and through your mouth," I told him, afraid he might throw up on my crime scene.

"He gonna be okay?" Slack asked.

"Oh, sure," I said. "He's not all the way used to the smells yet. This isn't nearly as bad as the lady who'd been eaten by her cats."

Slack rocked back on his heels again as he watched Sheldon pace back and forth like a caged tiger while he tried to get himself under control.

"I'm okay," Sheldon said, letting go of his shirt and taking off his glasses so he could wipe away the fog. "I'm good. Breathe through the mouth. Nice and slow and steady. I miss Lily. She always reminded me to breathe."

"I'm sure Blake can help you out with that," I said.

"Maybe," Sheldon said, not sounding convinced. "Maybe not. Did you know fewer than seventy thousand people in the United States are named Blake?" He said it as if the small number somehow made Blake less able to perform the task of reminding a person to breathe.

"Nope," I said. "Didn't know that one. And I'm not sure why you do."

"I looked it up after you introduced us," Sheldon explained. "I've never known a Blake before."

I wasn't sure Blake had even realized that his name had just been said several times and that we were talking about him as if he weren't standing right there. He wasn't quite the same shade of green Sheldon had been a couple of minutes ago, but his tan didn't look quite as healthy as when he'd first stepped into the ring.

"Whoa," Blake said, his eyes widening as he stared at the victim. "This is, like...definitely not the same as the cadavers in class. I put Vicks in my nose though so I'm not going to throw up or anything."

"That's always a plus," I said. It was an old body farm trick to put Vicks inside your nostrils to disguise the smell of decomposition or other post-mortem odors.

I noticed Sheldon hadn't taken his eyes off the victim once he'd gotten himself under control.

"Everything okay, Sheldon?" I asked.

"It's...it's Kaal Dracarian," Sheldon said, his voice higher pitched than usual. He patted his front pant pocket and then dug inside, coming out with an inhaler. He took a couple of huffs and then shoved the inhaler back in his pocket.

"Also known as Kevin Schwartzman," Jack said. "Our victim."

"Right," Sheldon said. "It's just...he looks so authentic. Look at the stitching on that cape. Fit for a king." Sheldon placed his fist over his heart.

"He's trippin'," Blake said, looking at Sheldon like he was from another planet.

"Let's get him bagged and back to the lab," I said before Sheldon could go into a full tribute for his fallen hero. "Go ahead and put him in the cooler. It's going to be a couple of hours before I get back. You can show Blake the protocols for transporting the body."

"I'm a fast learner, Doc," Blake said, giving me a blindingly white smile and a wink. "I'm number two in my class. I was hoping to get to shadow you so I could get a better feel for the full scope of the job. Maybe you and I can grab a cup of coffee later and I can show you some of my autopsy techniques."

Jack leaned his head toward me and said, "Is that today's version of showing someone your etchings?"

I pressed my lips together to keep from laughing and was really at a loss. I didn't want to crush the kid's ego, but I didn't have the time or inclination to deal with him.

"I'll get plenty of chances to see your techniques while you're interning," I said. "We're going to be very busy until we close this case. No one has a lot of time for coffee breaks when there's a body on the table."

Sheldon looked at me, confused. "You drink coffee all the time," he said. "Especially when you've got bodies on the tables. Emmy Lu got you that fancy new espresso machine for Christmas so you can work late at night." Then he turned to Blake and said, "She really drinks too much of the stuff. I don't think those levels of caffeine are healthy for anyone. Did you know that Americans drink a hundred and forty-six billion cups of coffee per year?"

"Really?" Blake asked, and Sheldon nodded like an eager puppy.

It was rare anyone showed interest when Sheldon spouted the endless facts stored in his brain, and I could tell he was about to start a long-winded conversation about all things coffee.

"Coffee talk later," I said and looked directly at Blake. "Sheriff Lawson and I have time for coffee breaks because it's what will keep us awake for the next forty-eight hours while we work this thing. Emmy Lu will show you where the coffeepot is back at the funeral home. Feel free to grab a cup during your break."

"Huh," Blake said, giving Jack a disapproving

glare. "I don't know about that, Dr. Graves. He looks dangerous."

"He is," I said. "That's why I married him. Now if you want to stay an intern, you and Sheldon need to get this body back to the lab." I ignored the surprised look in his eyes when he realized Jack was my husband and plowed ahead before there were any more delays. "Everything inside the body bag is evidence. Don't open it to look or touch once it's sealed. Sheldon will show you how to fill out and process the paperwork. Got it?"

"I've been waiting for this moment my whole life," Blake said eagerly. "I'm ready to get my hands dirty. I'll be the best intern you've ever had."

"Good," I told him. "Start with the paperwork and then let Sheldon and Emmy Lu show you around and go through the protocols. You need to be familiar with the rules of handling a victim before you can put your hands on him. And then go home and get a good night's sleep because our jobs are twenty-four seven until we find justice for the victim."

His smile deflated a bit. "I thought you already knew who killed him?"

"One of the first things you'll learn in this business is that nothing is ever as it seems."

I decided it was probably better to bag the victim myself. Sheldon had a look in his eyes that made me think he'd try to steal Kevin's costume if given the chance, and Blake was so eager to please there was no telling what he might do that could potentially compromise any evidence on the body. I really missed Lily. Her level of competence was hard to come by.

"Sheldon Durkus and Blake Steed, riding off into the sunset," I said once they'd rolled the victim to the Suburban waiting outside the doors of the arena.

"His name is Blake Steed?" Jack asked, giving me the side-eye. "No way someone named their kid that."

"Apparently, they did," I said.

"I'm suddenly a lot more worried about him being able to seduce you. A name like that has had some experience with the ladies."

"I'm fairly confident in my ability to ward off his advances," I said wryly.

"I'm going to run a background check on him," Jack said. "I don't trust him."

"Already done before he showed up on the crime scene," I said. "Let's go talk to Dwight Parr."

Jack held up the rope for me to crawl through and he followed me down the short steps to the basketball court floor.

"We'll keep you updated," Jack said to Chief Slack.

"I'd appreciate it," Slack said. "How do you want to handle the notification to the parents?"

Jack thought about it for a second. "I'll take care of it. Maybe they've got some information about Parr if he and Kevin were friends."

Slack nodded. "You're welcome to it," he said. "I

hadn't planned on making any more death notifications since I retired. I'd like to keep it that way. Y'all stay out of trouble."

We waved goodbye and made our way toward the athletic director's office.

"I'm going to have Carver run a deep check on your new intern," Jack said. "That kid has juvie written all over him."

"No way," I said. "He's all smarmy and entitled, but I don't see juvie."

"It's there," Jack said. "Want to put a wager on it? How about a hundred bucks?"

"A hundred bucks? That's a lot of money."

Jack's lips twitched. "I think you're good for it. What do you say? The kid's Eddie Haskell with a porn star's name. Do you know how dangerous that combination is?"

I stopped walking and stared at him. "First of all, no one Blake's age will have any clue who Eddie Haskell is. Second of all, are you jealous of a twenty-two-year-old entitled brat?"

"I've never been jealous of anyone in my life," he said. And I believed it. Jack had never had a self-esteem problem, and he'd never had to work very hard at getting or keeping a woman's attention.

"You don't have anything to worry about," I reassured him, finding the whole exchange amusing. "You keep doing that thing you did this morning and you're going to have me around another fifty or sixty years."

"On second thought, maybe I need to see if the kid will pitch in," he said. "You're wearing me out."

I elbowed him in the side and said, "Let's make it two hundred. A kid like Blake just needs a firm hand and direction."

"If you say so," Jack said. "But I'm having Carver run the deep check anyway."

The athletic director's office was in a corridor off the main entryway, past the ticket booths and turnstiles. Officer Plank had been assigned guard duty outside the door, and he was buttoned up in full uniform, not a wrinkle in sight.

I liked Plank. He was fresh out of the academy and still had a little shine on him that would eventually get tarnished with cynicism and distrust in another year or two.

"Hey, Plank," I said. "Long time no see."

"I've been working a lot of details over the holidays," he said. "Trying to save up."

"Oh, yeah?" I asked. "I heard through the grapevine that you and Wachowski were getting pretty serious."

His face turned scarlet all the way to the tip of his ears. "We...umm." Sweat dotted his upper lip and he looked back and forth between me and Jack.

"Geez, Plank," Jack said. "We're not your parents. Lighten up."

"Yes, Sheriff," he said, nodding. "Officer Wachowski and I have decided to move in together. We're saving up for a house."

"Gosh," I said, widening my eyes. "Isn't there a

rule about fraternizing with co-workers? Unless the two of you are just roommates, of course."

Plank somehow managed to turn even redder, and Jack just shook his head, his lips pressed into a hard line. "I guess we'll have to address this at your review."

It was hard to keep a straight face. Jack could lie like nobody's business. And as long as he wasn't lying to me, the skill came in handy from time to time.

"Of course," I said, looking at Jack. "There is the marriage clause, right Jack?" And then I turned back to Plank. "If y'all got married maybe your personal business wouldn't have to be paraded in front of the review board."

"I asked her to marry me," Plank burst out, panic in his eyes. "But she said no. She's a little gun shy about marriage. I've got to take baby steps. But maybe I can get her to change her mind."

I could practically see the wheels turning in Plank's head.

"Relax, Plank," Jack said, clapping him on the arm. "We're only teasing. As long as you both do your jobs, your business is your own. Does your mom know y'all are planning to move in together?"

With that jaw-dropping question, Jack moved past a paralyzed Plank and opened the door of the athletic director's office. That was the blessing and curse of living in a small town. Everyone knew everyone else's business, and Plank's parents were about as uptight and small town as you could get.

"Poor kid," I said, after the door was shut behind us. "Between his mother and Wachowski, he's not going to know whether to unzip his pants or run to the altar."

Jack nodded toward the hunched figure in the corner, staring aimlessly out the window. He looked like a boy—hunched in on himself and afraid. He was still dressed in costume, and his right hand was handcuffed to the desk chair he sat in.

"Dwight Parr?" Jack asked.

There was no response. Not even a flicker in his facial expression that he knew we were there.

I moved around Jack and sat across from Dwight on the padded window seat. I was a little taken aback by the professionalism of his makeup. The blue veins spreading from his neck and up his face looked real. A black wig lay on the desk, but Dwight still wore the wig cap, though it barely covered his reddish shock of natural curls. His eyes were a pale blue, and his pupils were barely a pinprick of black.

He showed classic signs of shock.

"I don't know, Jack," I said. "He might need to seek medical treatment before we get anything out of him."

I leaned forward so I could get in his direct line of sight and held up my fingers to see if he'd track with his eyes. He didn't.

"Dwight, I'm Dr. Graves," I said softly. "It's going to be okay. I'm going to take your pulse." His skin was pale and I reached out and took his wrist, placing my fingers over the sluggish pulse in his wrist. His skin was clammy and his movements were slow. "Do you know where you are?"

He blinked and his eyes stayed closed long enough I thought he'd fallen asleep. But then he opened them again and looked directly at me.

"Kevin," he said, his voice broken. "I killed Kevin."

CHAPTER THREE

I LOOKED AT JACK, BUT JACK'S EYES WERE NARROWED and there was a crease between his brows. The problem with being a cop was understanding that everyone was a liar and everyone had an angle. People mostly believe they're telling the truth, but they're telling the truth that generally paints them in the best light.

This wasn't our first murder case, and considering human nature, it wouldn't be our last. We'd sat across from some of the most violent and vicious killers one could imagine and watched as they lied convincingly right to our faces. I'd felt empathy and compassion for some of them, almost positive they were innocent until the evidence had piled up against them. I wasn't so quick to judge now.

The longer we did this job, the harder it was to trust anyone. The difference between me and Jack was my medical training. It was ingrained to take care of people first and ask questions later. But I'd learned in working with Jack that it was always the person in the body bag who had priority, and I could tell from the set look on his face that we'd be questioning Dwight Parr, come hell or high water.

I let out a quiet sigh and noticed the water-cooler over in the corner. "Maybe you could grab him a cup of water," I said.

Jack nodded and set the bagged sword down on the desk, and then came back seconds later with a paper cup of water.

"Dwight," I said. "Drink some water for me. We need to talk about Kevin."

"Kevin?" he asked. "I killed Kevin."

He looked down at the cup I was trying to wrap his fingers around and he noticed his other wrist was cuffed to the chair.

Jack took the seat next to me. "How did you kill Kevin?"

"I..." He stopped and stared at his water. "I don't know. My sword. It must have killed him. But the judges inspected it. It's never done that before." His head tilted and he was staring at something off in the distance.

"Dwight," Jack said, his voice hard enough that I winced. "Focus. What do you mean it's never done that before?"

"It's never done that," he said. "And it killed Kevin. I killed Kevin."

"Listen to me," Jack said. "Was Kevin your friend?"

"S...sure," he stuttered. "He was my suitemate freshman and sophomore year. My best friend."

"I'm going to ask you some hard questions and I need you to answer them truthfully so we can find out what happened to Kevin."

"Kevin's dead," Dwight said, and a single tear leaked from the corner of his eye.

"That's right," Jack said, nodding. "And Kevin deserves our best—to find out what happened to him. Accidents happen. But we all have to take responsibility for our actions."

Dwight gave a barely perceptible nod and made eye contact with Jack. "He was my friend."

"I believe you," Jack said. "What's your name?"

"Umm...Dwight," he said. "Dwight Parr."

"What's your major, Dwight?"

"Electrical engineering," he said. "Kevin would have won the match. He always does. My sword is no match for his axes. He even took fighting classes."

"You and Kevin have fought before?" Jack asked.

"Sure," Dwight said, finally taking a sip of water. "We're on the same live action Dungeons & Dragons team. We always act out our own fights. We all take our favorite video game character and then enhance it and give it a full story."

Color was coming back into Dwight's cheeks as he talked about his passion.

"How many of you are on the team?" I asked.

"Umm..." Dwight closed his eyes again. "Seven full-time players. Two part-time players who have temp characters written in whenever we need to expand the storyline."

I could practically hear Jack's thoughts. This was a level of nerd that far surpassed Sheldon.

"Why'd you kill Kevin?" Jack asked, switching up the questioning to keep Dwight off guard.

It worked, because Dwight crushed the paper cup in his hand and water spilled on the black leather pants he wore.

"I didn't...I mean...I was supposed to beat him. I wanted to win. But I didn't mean to kill him. I don't know what happened. It's never happened like that before. Kevin just stopped fighting and he stood there. And then he started twitching and I went in for the next blow. The more blows, the more points. I just wanted to win. I never win."

Jack took the plastic bag from the desk and opened it slowly so the hilt of the sword showed.

"No!" Dwight yelled, pushing his chair back to put space between himself and the sword. "Don't touch it! Don't touch it!" And then he leaned over and threw up on his pointed shoes.

Jack called for the EMTs and had Plank ride with Dwight to the emergency room to get checked out. Once he was stable Plank would bring him back to the sheriff's office and put him in holding so he could be questioned again.

We handed off the sword to the evidence tech,

and saw Chief Slack on our way back inside and he told us where we could find the event coordinator.

"What do you think about Dwight Parr?" I asked Jack as we took the elevator to the upper level where the press box was located.

Jack blew out a breath. "I have no idea. I feel sorry for the kid, but we need to talk to him sooner rather than later. I want to get a list of all the people in his D&D club, and I want to know if or how he enhanced that sword."

"Do you think he did it on purpose?" I asked.

"That's not for us to say right now," Jack said. "No matter what the circumstances, Dwight Parr killed another person. It's a homicide. Now whether or not it was murder is our job to figure out. We're going to have to hold him no matter what. Whether or not we charge him depends on what the evidence says."

"Yeah, yeah," I said, annoyed with the whole process. "But just for the record, I don't think he had a clue what was going to happen. That was a pretty visceral reaction back there."

"Lots of people react that way when they kill someone, especially after the first time," Jack said. "Either the excitement has to have an outlet, or maybe it wasn't what they expected it to be. Not everyone spends as much time around dead people as we do. A lot of people have never seen a dead person at all, much less one who was killed in such a horrific way. He'll have nightmares."

"There are going to be a lot of people having nightmares tonight," I said.

A woman came out of a narrow hallway right in front of us, and Jack and I both stopped in our tracks so we wouldn't run into her.

"That's why we've got counselors on standby to talk to any of the staff or students who might need extra help getting through this tragedy," she said.

She was a couple of inches shorter than I was with black hair cut in a sleek, chin-length bob, and gorgeous skin the color of espresso. Her lipstick was scarlet and matched her shoes and the silk shell beneath her black suit.

She held out a slim hand, and I noticed the gold wedding band on her finger, but it was the only jewelry she wore. She offered her hand first to Jack, and then to me.

"You must be Sheriff Lawson and Dr. Graves."

"And you are?" Jack asked.

"Elsa Taylor," she said, giving him a full-wattage smile. "Public relations. Is there anything I can help you with?"

"Ahh," Jack said. "We won't keep you from your work then. I'm sure you're very busy. We were told Trish Johnson is up here."

Elsa didn't let her smile slip at the easy dismissal. "She's right inside the press box with Dr. Coleman and our team. It's been a tragic day for everyone. Go right on in. They're expecting you. And please, let me know if I can be of any help."

"Thank you," Jack said, taking the card she offered. "We'll see ourselves in."

She nodded and moved around us, her heels clicking all the way to the elevator.

"She seems exhausting," I said as we moved toward the press box door.

Jack pulled on the handle and held it open so I could walk through, but I stopped just across the threshold and Jack had to move around me to get by. It felt like we were walking into a firing squad, and the chill in the air was palpable, though I had no idea why.

The room was big and open and was segmented into three arced desks that gave a bird's-eye view to the court below. Green chairs were lined behind the desks, and each space had a phone and a plug built right into the surface. Behind the desks was a long mahogany table, and five of the cushioned chairs were occupied by very serious-looking people—four men and a woman.

One of the men stood and said, "Jack, come on in and let me introduce you to everyone." He was in his mid-fifties, trim and in good shape. He wore a suit and a pair of horn-rimmed glasses that added to an already academic appearance.

Jack raised his brows and I could feel the tenseness in him, but he stood his ground. "Jim," Jack said. "I don't want to take up too much of your time. I just need to speak to you and your event coordinator for a few minutes and get a basic idea of what happened today."

"That's why we're here," Jim said. "We figured it was best to go ahead and get everything done here together since our attorneys are already on-site. Just to make sure everyone is protected. You understand, of course. Congratulations on the election win by the way," he said, his smile so fake I almost laughed out loud. "I haven't had a chance to see you since before the holidays. Rita and I were real proud to donate to your campaign."

Jack smiled, but it didn't reach his eyes. "Now, Jim, you're telling me you called in your attorneys for a formal interview when all I want to know are a few simple answers to a few simple questions. I just need a couple of minutes with both of you. A boy is dead, and the longer we stand around doing this, the longer it takes to find out what happened to him."

"Sheriff Lawson," one of the other men at the table said. "I'm John Horowitz with Lampman, Horowitz, and Crawford. Why don't you have a seat and we'll get this done so you can get back to work."

Jack's smile grew wider, and I resisted the urge to take a step back and out of the line of fire. Jack wasn't a fan of attorneys, and he especially wasn't a fan of attorneys trying to run the shots in an investigation.

"Well, Mr. Horowitz," Jack said, but he was looking at Jim Coleman. "I appreciate you trying to get things organized, but when I came in here, I was thinking I'd get cooperation from two employees of the university over the death of one of their students. But instead, those two employees have a troop of lawyers to do the talking for them, which leads me to believe that maybe there's something to hide and that maybe they're not so innocent after all. I mean, all I wanted was a list of rules for the tournament and a little background on the victim, but now I'm thinking I need to start digging a little deeper."

"Now hold on a second, Jack," Jim said, putting his hands up. "That's not what's happening at all. You know how these things work. This is the advice we were given, and we put these protocols in place for everyone's protection."

"I understand. You do whatever you need to do," Jack said. His tone was polite and friendly, and I knew he was about to drop the hammer. He turned back to Horowitz and said, "We'll need your clients at the sheriff's office at eight in the morning for formal interview." Then he looked at Jim and the scared-looking woman who hadn't made a peep. "Formal interviews can take hours. I hope these guys are worth what you're paying them."

The woman made a tiny gasp of outrage, and Jim went red in the face. "That's ridiculous, Jack."

"No, Jim," Jack said. "What's ridiculous is this power play for no reason whatsoever, when we've got a crime to solve and a family to let know that their child is dead. But by all means, make sure you tie things up in red tape."

"Fine," Jim said. "You three out. I'm not wasting my day tomorrow sitting at the sheriff's office."

"Dr. Coleman," Horowitz said, frowning at Jack.

"I don't want to hear it," Jim said, waving them away. "I took your advice and now I'm not. We don't have anything to hide. This was an accident. A tragic accident. There's nothing we could have done."

"Nothing you get from this interview will be admissible," Horowitz said.

"Wow," Jack said. "You really don't have a lot of faith in your clients. Maybe you want to go ahead and confess for them."

"Out," Jim said, staring Horowitz down with a steely glare.

The three attorneys gathered their legal pads and filed out of the room, not meeting our gazes. Jim came out from behind the table toward Jack and extended his hand.

"I'm sorry about that, Jack," Jim said, in full hospitality mode now. "You know how attorneys are. We just got caught up in it, but truly, we don't want to do anything to make things difficult for you and your wife." He turned to me and gave me a genuine smile. "Nice to see you again. We met at the Fourth of July party last year."

I wasn't nearly as good at remembering people's faces or names as Jack was, and it seemed I was always meeting someone or another at official events. For the life of me I couldn't recall having ever seen Jim Coleman before, but I nodded and gave him a friendly smile that I hoped gave the impression that I remembered our meeting fondly.

"Come on in and sit down," Jim said. "I don't know if you've met Trish Johnson, but she's the university event coordinator. You might have seen her at some of the donor receptions."

Trish looked like she was scared to death, but I'd learned over the years that some people just had that reaction to cops, no matter if they were innocent or guilty. She was a thin woman with high cheekbones and a long nose that spoke of a Native American ancestry somewhere down the line. Her dark hair was pulled up in a knot on the top of her head and a fringe of bangs rested above dark brows and thickly lashed black eyes. She was dressed casually in a KGU sweatshirt and jeans, and she looked young, too young to be a professor.

"Dr. Graves," I told her, extending a hand. Her skin was cold to the touch, but her handshake was firm.

"We won't take up much of your time," Jack said, holding out one of the rolling chairs for me to take a seat. "We know this is difficult for everyone on campus."

"That's an understatement," Jim said. "The last time we lost a student at this campus was eight years ago. A girl was hit by a drunk driver. This is a safe place. The phone is already ringing off the hook with panicked parents."

"I'm interested in the weapons that were used during the last match between Dwight Parr and

Kevin Schwartzman. We were told each of their weapons were inspected before they were allowed to fight."

Trish tapped her index finger repeatedly on the table in a nervous gesture, but she kept eye contact with Jack. "Believe me, I'm interested in knowing the answer to that too. None of this makes any sense. The weapons were inspected before the fight began."

"What about the enhancement?" Jack asked.

Her mouth pinched tight at that and she glanced at Jim. He let out a sigh and squeezed the back of his neck.

"Honestly, that's what all the hullaballoo was about with the attorneys," Jim admitted. "The kids add things all the time to their weapons. Light shows and bits of technology that make it look like something from a video game or movie. But it's always been amateur stuff. It's the blades and spikes and weapons that impale that have always been the concern for safety."

"Why did you say none of this makes sense?" I asked Trish. "You say that as if you're familiar with Kevin and Dwight and their weapons of choice."

"Because I am," she said, blowing out a frustrated breath. "I'm the university event coordinator, but I'm also a professor of American history, and I'm the faculty sponsor for the KGU D&D club. I've known Kevin and Dwight since they were freshmen. I've seen them fight with those weapons before."

"And you've never seen the electrical component to the sword?" I asked.

"Not like that," she said. "Dwight has made enhancements over the last four years as his knowledge and skill have grown. He's a brilliant student. But it's all been for show. Extra lights or sound effects. He won the Archimedes Fellowship and is headed to Oxford this summer."

"We're very proud of him," Jim cut in. "It's a huge coup for the school."

"Did you know something was off about the sword?" Jack asked Trish.

"Not really," she said. "At least not at first. Like I've said, I've watched these guys fight many times before. Kids like Dwight and Kevin don't always fit in. In fact, I'd venture to say they've never fit in anywhere until they came here. But the D&D club is a family. It's a bunch of like-minded people who love and take pride in what they do—the fight sequences, the costumes, the fan fiction and original stories told.

"When Dwight hit the switch on his sword the blue light danced up the entire length to the tip. It was very cool to see, and all I could think was that he'd done an amazing job with his enhancements. I mean, it was pretty good before, but you could still see the flaws in it. But this time…it really was top notch. CGI quality." She ducked her head down and grasped her fingers together tightly. And then she looked up with a guilty expression on her face. "I was really proud of him when I saw it."

"Was there any bad blood between Kevin and Dwight?" I asked.

"No." She shook her head. "None at all. I'm telling you, they were friends, and they both loved the craft. I'd almost guarantee that when Kevin saw Dwight's sword do that it took everything he had not to run over and nerd out over it. That's the kind of guys they were."

"How many students are in the club?" Jack asked.

"We've got ninety this year," she said. "Being a nerd is becoming cool, so we've seen our numbers increase every year. But they're divided into groups by talent and ability, like a rank structure. There's Kings, Nobles, Knights, and Peasants. Dwight and Kevin are both in the Kings class."

"Any animosity between the groups?" I asked.

"No, everyone wants to be a King," she said, "So they're all working to collect points not only in their sessions, but in tournaments like this. The more points they have the faster they move up. But it's very difficult to become a King...or Queen," she added. "There are two women in the Kings class."

"So taking Kevin out wouldn't have advanced anyone else into the Kings group," Jack said.

Trish nodded. "Right. Promotion relies on everyone's individual merit."

"Dwight told us there were seven in his group," I said.

"Yes," she said. "They also use a couple of the Nobles who aren't far off from becoming Kings when they need extra players to fill in the storyline. They're very serious about their sessions."

"We need the names of everyone in the group," Jack said.

Jim leaned forward and rested his elbows on the table, steepling his fingers. "Can I ask why? I mean, you've got Dwight red-handed. He's even on video."

"It's our job to look at every angle," Jack said, smiling and pushing his chair back to signal the meeting was over. "Dwight seemed just as surprised as everyone else that the sword electrocuted Kevin. Which means he's a liar, it was an accident, or..."

"Or what?" Jim asked.

"Or someone else enhanced the sword and let Dwight do the dirty work."

CHAPTER FOUR

"I NEED TO MAKE THE FAMILY NOTIFICATIONS BEFORE it gets any later," Jack said once we were finished with Trish and Jim. "The school hasn't released the name of the victim yet, but I'm sure the media will have it by the time they go on air for the ten o'clock news."

"I guess that's my cue to head back to the funeral home," I said.

"Chicken," he said.

"You betcha. Death notifications are my least favorite thing to do," I said. "I hated doing it when I worked in the ER, and I still hate it. I'd much rather deal with people's grief at viewings and funerals, once it's had time to soften a bit. Fresh grief is too hard to watch."

Jack grunted but didn't say anything. I knew it was hard for him too.

"So..." I said. "I'm guessing by the exchange you

just had with Jim that he's something of a friend of yours. The way he talked to you was very familiar."

Jack shrugged. "We're friendly," he said. "When you move in the same circles long enough and money is involved, you get to know the faces in the room. There's always an event or fundraiser. Or golf tournaments." Jack snorted his irritation. "There seems to be a never-ending supply of golf tournaments. Jim and I have played on the same team a few times."

"How come you don't do all these fundraisers and events now?" I asked, narrowing my eyes at him. "Are you shirking your duties as heir to the Lawson fortune?"

Jack laughed and bumped against me affectionately. "No, I'm not shirking my duties. It was never a necessity to go. My checkbook is presence enough. But as much as I hate it, this job is as much politics as it is law enforcement."

"I hate that part too," I said. "Which I guess was why Jim decided to remind you he donated to your campaign fund. I really don't like that about him. I'm hoping you're not planning on setting up any double dates soon with the Colemans because I'm not a fan of people who think they can buy other people."

Jack smiled and put his arm around me. I was surprised because we were making our way across campus back to his unit and he didn't generally show public displays of affection while we were on duty. But now that I thought about it, I was usually the one to shy away from public displays of affection and Jack had just conceded to my wishes. I leaned into him a little and could feel his surprise.

"I'm not a fan either," he said. "People like Jim only know how to do things one way to get results. I've never needed anyone's money to hold office, and money has never kept me from doing right for the victims we serve."

"It's so sexy when you're in superhero mode," I said. "I bet you'd make all the nerds tremble with fear."

"I certainly hope so," Jack said, pinching my side. "My gun has real bullets. We'll drive through and grab dinner and then I'll drop you at the funeral home. Otherwise, you'll forget to eat."

***

My mind was already on the victim as Jack drove through the taco place to get our dinner. I wasn't particularly in the mood for tacos, but I knew my body needed fuel. A standard autopsy took a couple of hours, and this definitely wasn't a standard autopsy.

By the time Jack turned onto Catherine of Aragon, I'd inhaled two tacos and I was looking down my shirt for shredded cheese that managed to end up in my bra instead of my mouth.

"How can you possibly be that messy?" Jack asked, eyeing the front of my shirt.

"Tacos are not car food. Everybody knows that,"

I said defensively, though I noticed Jack had managed to eat his without a crumb in sight.

He pulled into the driveway and parked behind my Suburban. "Good luck with the autopsy," he said, helping me brush off a few stray crumbs.

"Good luck with the family." I leaned over and gave him a quick kiss and jumped out of the Tahoe, grabbing my medical bag from the back seat.

There were cars in the staff parking lot, and I remembered that we had a viewing starting at seven. A viewing of which I was supposed to be in attendance.

Since Sheldon had come on full time we'd worked out a schedule where we alternated our evenings and weekends for the most part, but when I had to put on my coroner hat, Sheldon was the one who had to fill in. Especially now that Lily was gone. But at least Emmy Lu was there as backup in case Sheldon needed to be rescued from normal conversation.

I went in through the side door under the carport and waved bye to Jack as he backed away. I locked the door behind me, hung my medical bag on the hook, and then went into the kitchen to start a pot of coffee.

I was procrastinating, and that wasn't like me. I'd had a lightning strike victim come through the ER when I'd been a doctor for the living, and I'd never forgotten the damage Mother Nature had inflicted on the fragile human body. It had been one of the few times over the course of my career

I'd had nightmares. And I wasn't sure why. I'd certainly seen more gruesome victims, but there'd been something about the helplessness of an attack like that—completely unexpected—that had haunted me.

Two women had been walking home from work, chatting about everyday things and trying to beat the incoming storm, at least according to the one who'd survived. The storm had been a good ways in the distance, or so it seemed, and then one of them dropped their phone in a storm drain. It had saved her life. Because while she was on the ground trying to reach her phone, the other was standing beneath a metal awning using her own phone to call her friend so she could see the phone light up in the darkness and pinpoint the location. One strike of lightning from the sky was all it took to catapult the woman into the empty baseball field across the street. She'd been dead in an instant.

But I had a feeling Kevin Schwartzman hadn't been dead in an instant. There had been topical burns that looked as if they'd spread across the skin. It hadn't been a direct hit from a single bolt.

I was lost in thought, watching the coffee drip slowly into my cup, so I was startled when someone came up close behind me and tapped me on the shoulder.

"Oh, Blake," I said, taking a step back. "I didn't know you'd still be here."

"I called your name, but I guess you were

thinking about something else," he said, giving me a sympathetic smile.

"Yeah, I guess I was," I said. "You can go on home. There's a viewing tonight and people will start showing up soon. There's nothing for you to do quite yet."

"I was hoping I could observe you in the lab," he said. "That's why I hung around."

I opened the fridge to get the cream, and when I closed it again it felt like he was standing closer.

"I don't think so," I said sharper than I meant, so I softened it by saying, "I've got a long night ahead of me, and most of my time is going to be spent preparing the body. There's a possibility I might not get to the autopsy until tomorrow, and if that's the case then you can observe. But tonight it's going to be a lot of tedious prep work."

I moved to get my cup from the Keurig and add cream, and I felt him shift closer again. Little red flags were starting to go off in my brain, and I grabbed my cup and the carton of creamer and moved to the island, but he followed.

"I really don't mind the tedious work," he said, moving in close again. "I've found I excel in seeing to the details."

He rested his hand on my hip, and I think it was the audacity of the move that had my mouth dropping open in shock and my feet feeling like there was lead in my shoes.

"Have you been drinking?" I asked, appalled.

He chuckled and his fingers squeezed against

the flesh at my hip. "Nothing but coffee. I swear." The way he said it was as if we were a part of some inside joke, only he was the only one on the inside. I was somewhere in the Twilight Zone.

"You're going to want to move your hand right now," I said, my words slow and deliberate. "And then you're going to want to take a step way back."

He laughed as if I'd told the most hilarious joke he'd ever heard. "Don't be a tease, Jaye. I saw how you were looking at me today. I know when a woman wants me, and I could see it in your eyes. The eyes never lie. But I also knew you could never make the first move. It wouldn't be professional. So many lawsuits and complaints nowadays about fraternizing with employees.

That was fast thinking on your part to let me know you were with your husband today. But don't worry. I know how to keep a secret."

I felt the color drain from my face and took a step back out of his grasp, but again, he followed.

"I think you're done here," I told him, grasping his wrist before he could touch me again. "I'll call Dr. Helmlich in the morning and let him know things aren't going to work out for you as an intern."

"Stop playing coy, Jaye," he said. "The chase is fun for a little while, but we're both adults, and I've been thinking about this moment since I was given the opportunity to choose where I wanted to do my internship. There's a lot of information about you online. And I knew we'd be a perfect fit. Like I said, I know when a woman wants me."

"Somehow, I don't think you do," I said stiffly.

"I'm an up-front kind of guy," he said, gaze narrowing, and the mean coming into his eyes. Just in that one glance I could see exactly what Jack had been talking about. This kid was trouble.

"I don't like to play games," he said, his smile sharp. "I'm taking you up on your offer. We're here right now, and everyone else is busy. I saw you have an office back there. Why don't we move somewhere more comfortable?"

He stepped into me again, and I let go of his wrist so I could move freely. I could feel the tightness in my chest and the anxiety taking hold. I'd been attacked before. Felt the powerlessness of being held down while the life had been choked out of me. And I knew I couldn't go through that again. Not and keep my sanity.

"First of all," I said, trying to keep my voice smooth so he couldn't hear the fear. "You've got to be some kind of moron to make a move like this on a cop's wife. And second, if you touch me again, I'm going to break your face. Maybe I didn't make myself clear the first time, but you're fired. You're done here. I don't want to see you anywhere near me again."

His face flushed red and he exploded with anger. "You're the one who came on to me! You think anyone is going to believe your poor little me routine? Like you didn't want this? You probably have a whole string of interns you jerk around and tease, but not me, you bitch." He moved in fast so I was trapped against the island, and his pelvis was pressed hard against mine. "I don't put up with that crap from any woman."

I brought the back of my wrist up hard under his chin, snapping his teeth together, and then I immediately followed through with a knee to his groin and a jab in his gut hard enough to knock the wind out of him. I quickly moved to the opposite side of the island and wrapped my shaking hands around my forgotten coffee mug. My cell phone was in my pocket, and I toyed with the idea of calling 911, but I didn't want to cause a scene for the family who was coming soon to honor their loved one.

"Well, that was entertaining," Emmy Lu said, coming in the kitchen to stand beside me. She put her hand on my back and stroked in soothing circles. "Makes you wonder how many women he's tried that same routine on. Good thing I was standing right there watching the whole thing. Other women probably weren't so lucky as to have a witness that would have no problem helping you hide his body right now."

I'd already had the same thought. If Blake was bold enough to try this with me, he had probably wreaked havoc across campus with less-experienced girls. Boy, had Jack won that two hundred dollars fair and square.

"Listen up, Blake," I said. "You're an entitled

creep, and you're about to find out what it's like to have law enforcement watching your every move. How many women have you forced yourself on? How many complaints are we going to find once we start digging?"

He was hunched over, grasping the edge of the island, but he managed to shoot me a daggered glare.

"I'm guessing we're going to find a pattern," I said. "Men like you make me sick, and jail is too good for you. Maybe you'll think about your bruised balls the next time you try to pull something like this. And if you don't think about it, maybe you'll get lucky and the next woman will slit your throat instead of using her fists."

"No one..." he gasped for air, "...will believe you."

"Wow," Emmy Lu said. "He sure thinks he's something special. I'm going to ask my son what that's called. He's a psychology major. I'm thinking Romeo here is pretty textbook."

"Leave," I said, staring him down. "And don't ever come back."

He muttered something unflattering, but I was past the point of caring. There were about to be a whole lot of people here in a short amount of time, and I was tired of making front page news for scandals.

Jack and I were still reeling from the bombshell Floyd Parker had leaked to the media about the son Jack had fathered when he'd been nineteen. Politics was a dirty business, and it was as dirty as it got when Floyd decided to run against Jack for sheriff. Fortunately, the people of King George hadn't been swayed by Floyd's tactics. But having another breaking news story so close to the last one wouldn't be good. Jack and I had both gotten too much media attention over the last year, and I, for one, was tired of it, especially since it tended to bring the crazies out of the woodwork.

Emmy Lu and I watched as Blake sucked in a deep breath and managed to stand all the way upright, and then he shuffled out through the kitchen door and slammed it behind him. We both let out a shuddering breath.

"You okay, honey?" Emmy Lu asked.

I inhaled deeply again and then exhaled slowly. "Yeah, I'm okay. Thanks for not killing him."

"I gotta tell you," Emmy Lu said. "This is about the most exciting job I've ever had. There's never a dull moment."

"I wouldn't mind having some dull moments every once in a while."

"Give me that cup," she said. "I'll make you some fresh coffee. Your hands are still shaking. I swear when I saw him all pressed up against you like that I was about to rush in and smash him over the head with the blender. I'm glad I didn't have to though. That blender makes real good smoothies."

Emmy Lu took the cup from my hands and dumped the coffee in the sink. She didn't bother to mess with the Keurig this time but went straight to the espresso machine for the serious stuff. I took the opportunity to grab a bottle of water and dig the aspirin out of the drawer, and then I sat back and watched efficiency in motion.

Emmy Lu had been with me the last year, and I didn't know how I'd ever gotten along without her. She was a dozen years older than me, and had babysat me a time or two in my youth. But she'd gotten married right out of high school and had five boys before she turned twenty-five and threatened to perform the vasectomy on her husband herself.

When her youngest had graduated high school, her husband had taken all their money, the barely legal receptionist at the tax office, and filed for divorce before hightailing it to Florida. Emmy Lu had been a stay-at-home mom for her entire adult life, and she looked like Gidget with crow's-feet.

She'd needed a job, and I'd finally been in a position to hire a receptionist. She'd been fresh off the divorce when I'd hired her but she'd recently been spending a lot of time at the Donut Palace with Tom Daly, and she was spending so much time there the rumor around town was that she and Tom were making more than donuts.

"I've got to get downstairs and get to work," I said. "I'm just making my night longer."

"Well, take this down with you," Emmy Lu said, pressing the cup in my hand. "Sheldon and I have everything under control for the viewing tonight."

"Thank you," I said, leaning against her in a

half hug. "I know this is outside of your job description."

"Honey, just about everything I do here is outside my job description," she said. "I get to do all the normal boring stuff at home. Do you know how much laundry I've done in my life with five boys? I'll take a night with Sheldon and a dead body any day of the week."

"That must be a lot of laundry," I said.

The lab was always cold, but tonight it seemed colder, and I pulled on a University of Virginia sweatshirt before putting on my lab coat. Most of the labs in the state weren't as advanced as mine. It was probably the only thing I could thank my parents for. Their criminal activity caused them to need top-notch equipment, and the same criminal activity paid for it all.

It was white and sterile, like a good lab should be. I never wanted to make it feel too cozy because I already spent enough time here. There were two stainless-steel embalming tables in the center of the room—after all, that was the main function of the lab—and a body cooler large enough to hold six ran along the back side of the room.

I had the autopsy table closest to my desk and workstations because there was so much back and forth with paperwork, x-rays, and tox reports. I grabbed my lab coat and put it on top of the sweatshirt and buttoned it up, and then I put on a heavy canvas apron. I'd learned the hard way to never wear your best clothes to an autopsy.

I scrolled through my phone until I found my music app and decided on Ella Fitzgerald to keep me company. I slid open the door of the cooler and rolled Kevin Schwartzman to the autopsy table. He wasn't a big man, so it didn't take much to move him from the gurney onto the table. I blew into my latex gloves and slipped them on.

"Okay, Kevin," I said. "Let's see what happened to you."

The motorized lift straps hung above the table. I pressed the button to lower them. I unzipped the black bag and fixed the straps beneath him so I could remove him from the bag without losing any potential evidence. Anything that fell off the body would just drop into the bag.

I hit the button again and Kevin lifted far enough into the air that I could remove the body bag from beneath him. I took another set of photographs with the lights on bright, paying close attention to the scorched flesh and melted metal of the chain mail around his head and chest. The electricity had found its exit route through the nose, chin, and fingers for the most part, but the toes of his boots had been blown out and blackened toes peeked from behind the charred leather.

I'd worked burn victims before, but this wasn't the same. Kevin had enough salvageable tissue to do a full autopsy. I'd thought through all the ways to best remove the melted bits of chain mail from his skin. It was worse than I'd originally thought, and no matter what I did, the epidermis would be destroyed. There was no saving it for analysis. I could either spend hours trying to come up with a diluted acid solution to remove it bit by bit, or I could remove the layer of skin and metal completely with my scalpel.

With the decision made, I removed the clothing I could and hung everything up to be examined later, documenting each piece on the autopsy form I'd started for Kevin Schwartzman. I found his wallet and cell phone in a hidden pocket inside his jacket. I tried to turn the phone on, but it had been fried along with the rest of him. I bagged them both for Jack, figuring someone could get the data from the phone later.

The exposed skin was scarlet and looked badly sunburned, and I could see the blue of his veins from underneath. I started with the chain mail on his chest, using my forceps to pull the chain mail in an upward direction, and then I carefully slid my scalpel beneath it, separating the two. It was a painstaking process since he'd worn a full chain mail shirt. I didn't know much about chain mail, but I was guessing it was expensive. Cheap metals would've melted much differently. If I had to guess, this chain mail would've held up well during battle a couple of centuries ago.

I used the lift to turn him and keep him suspended while I repeated the procedure on his shoulders and back, and by the time I made it up the back of his neck, the last song on my playlist was fading away.

There was a buzz and the click of the lock, and for a split second, fear gripped me and I grasped the scalpel in my hand a little tighter. I'd spent the last couple of years with my father popping up like a weed whenever he felt like it, and that fear of the unknown had only started to fade after his death. But in reality, I'd lived a good part of my life in fear —fear of being alone, fear for my life, fear for Jack's life—and I'd finally decided to take control over the last several months.

But the incident with Blake had shaken me more than I'd realized, because it had been his face I'd been expecting when the door opened. And then I felt stupid because after everything I'd been through and after overcoming so much, in an instant I was filled with anxiety just as I had been before.

Jack appeared in the doorway, and I let out a slow, shaky breath and relaxed my grip on the scalpel, laying it down on my equipment tray.

"Hey," I said, pulling off my gloves and tossing them in the trash. I glanced at the clock and realized I'd been at it a couple of hours already, and I removed the heavy apron and hung it on a peg. "I wasn't expecting to see you here tonight."

I covered Kevin with a white sheet up to the waist and went to the mini-fridge and grabbed a couple of waters. I listened to Jack's footsteps as he came down the stairs, but he didn't say anything.

It wasn't until I saw his face that the realization hit me. White lines of anger creased around his mouth and eyes, and I knew what he was going to say before it left his mouth. I'd blown it. Big time.

CHAPTER FIVE

"I'M SORRY," I SAID, COMING AROUND THE TABLE TO meet him. "I should have called you. I wasn't thinking."

Some of the anger deflated from him and I could see the hurt behind it. I hated when I hurt Jack, even unintentionally. But I should have been the one to call and tell him about Blake.

"Emmy Lu called me," he said. "She didn't want you left here by yourself at night with that nutjob running around. Her words, not mine. I've got much better words to describe him."

"Hmm," I said. "Well, I guess I'm glad one of us was thinking clearly. I completely put it out of my mind. I don't think I could've functioned tonight if I hadn't. He surprised me more than anything, but I handled it. And I'm going to call the dean of the department in the morning and file a formal complaint with the university."

"That's not all you're going to do," Jack said.

"You're going to press charges with the sheriff's office too. Guys like this are a dime a dozen. It needs to go on his record because he'll do it again. If we make life harder for him maybe he'll think twice before he does it to the next woman."

I blew out an uneasy breath. "I know you're right," I said, handing him a bottle of water. I didn't touch him yet. He had that stiff look about him that said he wasn't quite ready to let go of his anger. "I've got no excuse. I am sorry. All I can say is that I was thinking about Kevin's autopsy, and then Blake showed up out of nowhere. It was easier to focus on Kevin than think too hard about what happened."

Jack blew out an aggravated breath and pulled me into his arms. "The only reason that makes any sense to me is because I know you well. But just so we're clear, if he shows up anywhere around you again I'm going to rearrange his face and enjoy it."

"Good," I said. "I threatened him with you. What kind of dummy does something like that to a cop's wife?"

"An entitled brat who's never been told no," he said. "And just in case, I'm hanging here with you until you're ready to go home."

"Wow," I said. "You must be worried about me. You hate being down here."

"Only when you're embalming," he said. "It takes days to get the smell out of my nostrils, and I have to throw my clothes away."

I snorted out a laugh. "Not to mention it makes you throw up. It's kind of weird to think of some of the crime scenes we've been to, and the only thing that turns your stomach is the smell of embalming fluid. That's messed up."

Jack rolled his eyes and released me. "Found anything interesting with the victim?"

"I'm still removing the melted chain mail from his skin," I said. "You want to talk about smells..."

"Let's not," he said.

I went over to my workstation and grabbed the evidence bag with the phone and wallet inside and gave it to Jack.

"These were on the inside pocket of his jacket," I said. "Phone is dead. It was probably fried along with our victim."

"I've got a warrant to examine anything retrieved from the body, but I'll give it to the tech guys and see what they can pull from it." He got a pair of gloves from the box on my desk and opened the bag, taking out the wallet. It was a standard brown leather wallet that looked like it had seen better days.

"You have an extra scalpel?" Jack asked. "It's stuck together."

"Sure," I said, handing him an older one from the drawer.

He sat down at my desk and carefully started deconstructing the wallet. The plastic cards and pockets had melded together. Since Jack had something to occupy himself, and since he seemed to be done talking about the incident with Blake, I decided to go back to removing the rest of the chain mail from Kevin's head.

I started another playlist—this one of Billie Holiday—and I grabbed another pair of gloves, put my apron back on, and grabbed a new scalpel. I'd have to remove hair along with flesh and wanted a fresh blade. I hummed along with the music as I finished the task, and when I was done I held up the chain mail shirt with the attached hood and then laid it flat on an evidence table.

"That's disgusting," Jack said, looking up from the cards and money he had spread out in front of him.

"The human body is a fascinating thing," I said. "So many intricacies and layers. Nerve endings and tissue and muscles and bones. When everything is working in accordance it's a beautifully and wonderfully made machine. But if you throw in an extra element..."

"Like electricity?" Jack asked.

"Yes, like that," I agreed. "You throw in an added element and it ruins every part of the system. That chain mail he was wearing and the metal on his jacket and cape. It's like his body was trapped in a big microwave."

"I watched the tape Chief Slack gave me," Jack said. "From the time the sword first made contact with Kevin, it was almost two minutes before he dropped to the ground and Dwight and the ref ran over to check on him."

"That's a long and painful amount of time to be

microwaved," I said, sorrow pressing against my chest at the thought of what Kevin had gone through. "Anything in the wallet?"

"Seven dollars, driver's license, a credit card, a membership card to the National Comic Book Association, and one of those photo booth pictures of him and a girl."

"A girlfriend?" I asked.

Jack looked at me with brows raised. "I'm thinking a sister or cousin. She's very pretty, and he doesn't strike me as the type to understand that there are beautiful women outside of those weird video games and anime shows."

"Hmm, good point. Poor kid." I turned off the music and peeled my gloves off again, tossing them in the trash. Now that I'd stripped Kevin to the skin I had to take another set of photos, documenting everything from birthmarks to tattoos. I looked back at Jack. "I'm just getting started on this. Are you sure you want to stay? It'll be a couple of more hours."

He looked at me out of dark, irritated eyes. "I'm staying. I want to know where Blake Steed is and what he's doing. I told you earlier I was calling in a favor to Carver to run a deep background check on him, and I've got Martinez doing a visit to his apartment to make sure he's where he's supposed to be."

"Is that the only favor you called in to Carver?" I asked, raising a brow. "You didn't happen to mention our current crime scene?"

Ben Carver was Jack's best friend. Jack had lived

an interesting and varied law enforcement career, and somewhere along the way Jack had been involved with the FBI and the government on a level that far outranked my security clearance, not that I had one to begin with.

Jack had saved Carver's life at some point, and they'd been inseparable ever since. I still didn't know exactly what Carver's position was within the FBI, but from an outsider's point of view it seemed like he was a valuable asset and didn't really have to answer to anyone but the FBI director himself.

My father had almost killed Carver several months ago by running him off the road, and the crash had left Carver with not much more than a body full of broken bones and a stubbornness that kept him coming back to life on the operating table. Or maybe Carver's wife and four daughters had been all the will he'd needed to live. It had been a long and slow recovery, and he was still wheelchair bound and going to intense physical therapy several times a week. There was still a chance Carver might never walk again, but if I was a betting woman, I'd put my money on Carver. Not many people had as hard of a head as he did.

Jack grinned. "It turns out Carver knows a thing or two about these tournaments and the players."

"You think?" I asked sarcastically. "He's probably the head dungeon master controlling all the lesser dweebs."

I used makeup wipes to take off the remaining makeup on Kevin's face, and I finished taking photographs, noting that Kevin had no identifying marks on his body, at least not on the skin that hadn't been removed. I turned on my recorder and went through the process. I'd learned to back up my written records with a recording. Red tape and bureaucracy sometimes let evidence and other important things fall through the cracks.

"Victim is identified as Kevin Schwartzman," I said. "Age twenty-one. Caucasian male. Hair and eyes are reddish-blond and brown. No identifying marks on the body."

I put on a fresh set of gloves and went about measuring and weighing him, and then I ran a full set of x-rays.

"Childhood fracture of the tibia," I said, looking at the x-rays. "Slight curvature of the spine, indicating scoliosis."

I did a more thorough inspection of any remaining fingernails and toenails, and I used my light and magnifier to search for needle marks or anything that might indicate drug use. But Kevin Schwartzman looked like your average kid who spent too much time indoors and in front of a screen.

"We know Dwight delivered the killing blow," Jack said, once I was finished. "But we're running with multiple scenarios. Either Dwight did it on purpose and he's an excellent actor."

"Which means we need to dig deep for a motive," I said.

"Right," Jack agreed. "Or it was a total freak

accident and Dwight didn't realize the alterations to his sword basically turned it into a cattle prod."

"Which is also a possibility," I said.

"Or scenario number three, Dwight was just an easy weapon for the real killer. What better way to get away with murder than to have someone else do it in a room full of thousands of people?"

"And if that's the case," I said. "We have no suspects and no motive."

"Bingo," Jack said.

I put on a surgical mask and said, "I'm not sure I'm going to have anything exciting or new to tell you when I'm done here." I made the first incision for my Y-cut. "Get anything from the parents?"

Jack re-bagged the wallet and its contents and got up to get another bottle of water, and then he moved to the secondary desk I had on the back side of my main workstation where I kept a laptop.

"Nothing of interest," Jack said. "I talked to the mom and stepdad. They took it like you'd expect. Kevin is their youngest of three."

"So maybe the girl in the picture isn't a sibling," I said, intrigued.

"They've met Dwight on several occasions, along with the rest of the group. I guess during the summer and Christmas breaks they do some of their D&D sessions at their parents' houses since they can't use campus spaces. They weren't aware of any issues or troubles between Kevin and Dwight, or any of the kids for that matter."

I breathed out slowly into my mask and said,

"Of course not. That would be too easy. Who are you going to have take that sword apart?"

"Carver had an idea about that," Jack said.

He didn't say anything for several minutes, and I was focused on removing and weighing organs. Once I was done I said, "And what was Carver's idea?"

"Doug," he said.

I looked up sharply and said, "You're kidding. He's kidding. That's insane."

"That's Carver," Jack said, shrugging.

"Doug is a teenager," I said.

He was also a genius and Carver's nephew, and he'd helped us with cases before. But he was something of a wild card, and he wasn't as disciplined as Carver as far as not flaunting his rule breaking. Which was why he'd spent the first couple of his teenage years under house arrest and unable to leave the state because he'd gotten caught hacking into the Pentagon.

"That sword could be dangerous in the wrong hands," I said. "You really want to hand it over to Doug?"

"Oddly enough, I feel safer with it under his care than any of the tech guys in local law enforcement."

I narrowed my eyes at Jack. "He's not living with us is he?"

Jack smiled tightly. "Look on the bright side, the house will be stocked with all your favorite junk foods."

"He eats everything in sight," I said. "We'll have to hide our food in the bedroom closet again."

"Not me," Jack said, looking smug. "I like adult food. Like fruits and vegetables. Doug never touches my stuff. Maybe you should make a change to your diet."

"That'll be a cold day in hell," I muttered under my breath. I'd managed to live a lot of years on my juvenile diet, and I was content to continue. It's not like I didn't eat fruits and vegetables. But when given the choice of green beans or a moon pie, the moon pie was going to win every time.

"Are you almost done?" Jack asked, getting up to stretch his legs and back.

"I just have to put Humpty Dumpty back together again, and then you'll have your case file," I said.

"Nice," Jack said, wincing at my terminology.

"There's no drugs or alcohol in his system. The contents of his stomach consisted of soda, a candy bar with chocolate, peanuts, caramel, and nougat, pepperoni pizza, and two breath mints."

"Appetizing," Jack said. "That changes my mind about grabbing a midnight snack. Anything interesting about cause of death?"

"Official cause of death is electric shock," I said. "But I did find something interesting when I started looking at his organs."

"What's that?" Jack asked, coming over to the autopsy table.

"They weren't damaged," I said. "I mean, not at

all. When a victim is struck by lightning, the volts are strong enough to damage not just the tissue to the body as it looks for an outlet, but it travels inside the body as well, destroying everything in its path. But there is no damage to any of his organs. It's all external."

"Which means what?" Jack asked.

"Which means that if Kevin hadn't been wearing all that metal armor for the electrical current to get trapped in, basically cooking his body, then I think he very well would have survived."

CHAPTER SIX

THERE WAS SOMETHING ABOUT HOME THAT MADE THE day fall away as soon as I stepped through the door. It wrapped around me like a warm hug and made me want to curl up and stay there forever, never having to see another living soul outside of my own space. Even as I lay awake in the dark, Jack's soft breathing steady next to me, I felt the safety and comfort of home.

It had only been home for a short while, but it felt as if I'd never lived anywhere else. It was the first place I felt I'd belonged. The first place I'd felt safe. The first place I'd been part of a real family.

Even after the house had been destroyed by my parents and our sanctuary had been breached, it was still the only place I ever wanted to be.

The weatherman had been right about the snow getting worse through the night. It was a full moon, and I could see the fast-falling flakes through the floor-to-ceiling windows that covered the west wall. The treetops were completely white, and the wind howled.

I wasn't normally a morning person, but sleep hadn't come easily, and when it had come it had been filled with dreams—dreams of Jeremy Mooney with his hands around my throat that had morphed into images of Blake Steed staring at me with evil red eyes as he finished the task Jeremy Mooney hadn't been able to.

I'd woken in a cold sweat, my heart thudding heavily in my chest, and Jack had murmured something and wrapped his arm around me, pulling me close before he fell back asleep.

His touch had helped soothe me, but sleep was elusive, so I watched the darkness change hues and the shadows shift, until the snow glared off the light of the moon and cast a bluish tint into the room so I could see every detail as if it were daylight.

It would be another twenty minutes before the alarm went off and Jack woke up, so I decided to slip out of bed and bring him his coffee instead of the other way around like usual.

"Still awake?" he asked, squeezing me tighter, as if he knew I was about to leave him.

"I was just about to go down and start the coffee," I said.

"Mmm, I could get used to that." He took my hand and played with the band on my finger, twisting it back and forth. "What's wrong?"

I let out a soft sigh. This was one of those marriage things. My knee-jerk reaction was to tell him that nothing was wrong and to go about my day. But that wouldn't have been the honest answer and he would've known it. I was still getting used to having a partner I could rely on, someone to share my burdens with.

"Nightmare," I said. "I haven't had them in a long time. It doesn't take a psychologist to know that what happened with Blake triggered the dream, but it brought back other memories and now they're floating at the surface. I keep seeing Jeremy Mooney's face, and then it changes into Blake's. Only this time no one stops him from squeezing that last bit of life from me."

Jack tucked me even tighter against him and rested his chin in the crook of my neck.

"Jeremy Mooney is dead," Jack reminded me. "And even though I'd love to promise you that I'll always be there to fight the bad guys for you, I know that's a promise easily broken. But don't let a jerk like Blake Steed take away your power. If he takes away your power then he'll own you. I've seen you stand up against the enemy. I've watched you fight for your life. Jeremy Mooney came close to killing you but he didn't succeed, and when you came back from that the fight that lives inside you was still there. He didn't kill it. It emboldened you. It made you brave when others would've have lived in fear. You learned to fight. You learned to shoot. And you're prepared if the need ever arises. It's smart to have a healthy dose of fear. It'll keep you vigilant. But you can't let it cripple you."

"I know," I said. "I was just...surprised, I think. I haven't dreamed about Jeremy Mooney since right after the incident. I thought I'd put all that behind me. I thought I'd learned to identify those triggers that could spark things like nightmares or anxiety attacks. I guess I'm more disappointed in myself than anything that I let it creep up on me like that."

"There's no shame in having a reaction to what Blake did to you," Jack said. I could hear the anger in his voice again as if he was hearing about the assault for the first time. "I'd be worried if you didn't have a reaction. Now you know the kind of man he is. Now you have the knowledge you need to protect yourself and make wise decisions regarding your safety. It's better to have a good picture of the kind of person you're dealing with than be bit by a snake in the grass."

"I know you're right," I said. "Thanks, Jack. This marriage stuff is pretty handy from time to time."

He chuckled and pinched my hip. "I'm glad you're getting your money's worth. You've got a little time before the alarm goes off. Why don't you try to get some more sleep?"

My eyelids were already heavy and I felt myself fading into sleep. Jack's lips touched my ear and he snuggled in behind me.

It was the smell of coffee that woke me sometime later. Jack had lowered the blackout shades on the windows, so I had no idea how long I'd been asleep, and I grappled on the nightstand for my phone so I could see the time.

It was already past eight, and though I wanted to groan at my late start on the day, I was glad for the sleep. I could see the steam from the coffee mug, so I knew it hadn't been sitting there long.

I tossed back the covers and put my feet on the floor, feeling much better than I'd expected to feel after the night I'd had. I wasn't a morning person in general, and I wasn't even hospitable until after the first cup of coffee, so I took the cup from the nightstand and shuffled my way into the bathroom, hitting the switch on the wall to open all the blinds.

Jack had already been in and showered, and he'd made sure the floor tiles and towel rack were heated for my benefit. I stepped in the shower with my coffee and then saw the shadow out of the corner of my eye.

"I figured you'd have already left for the office," I said, taking a sip of coffee and feeling the first jolt of caffeine run through my system. Sheldon was probably right. I probably did drink too much coffee. But there were some things I wasn't willing to compromise on. As far as I was concerned, it was a health risk to others.

"We got more snow last night than forecasted, so everything is delayed while the streets are being cleared. Most of the schools and businesses in the county are getting a late start. One of the guys will be here in a little while so you can have formal charges brought against Blake, and then once the campus opens back up, I figure we'll head over to KGU and talk to the names on the list of the D&D club."

At the mention of filing a formal complaint I felt my lungs constrict. Why was that my reaction? Blake deserved to have charges brought against him. If not for me then for some other woman. But there was a part of me that was hesitant. I didn't know if it was because I was ashamed it had happened at all and didn't want anyone to know, or if I was afraid Blake's boasts might be true that no one would believe me.

"That works," I finally said, deciding that whether I was comfortable or not, it had to be done. "We don't have any funerals on the books today, so I'm not needed at the funeral home. Emmy Lu and Sheldon can handle things. Though I am going to give Lily a call and see if I can bribe her into taking a part-time job while she's doing her doctoral work."

"Don't forget Doug is going to show up at some point today," Jack said. "I want him working on that sword as soon as possible. That's going to be the key to this whole thing."

I stepped out of the shower and Jack handed me one of the warmed towels. "Thanks," I said and wrapped it around me.

"I'll meet you in the office in a few," he said, tugging at the towel playfully. "I'm expecting a call from Carver."

I grunted and went about my morning routine. I looked at myself in the mirror and noted the darkened circles under my eyes, but that was nothing concealer couldn't fix. The past couple of months had been difficult ones, and I was thinner through the face so my cheekbones were more pronounced. I was naturally thin with a long, athletic build, and I didn't have much to speak of in the hips and bust —even less so now.

The good thing about having shorter hair was the drying time, so I ran my fingers through it and blasted it with hot air until it was dry, and then I put on moisturizer and concealer, figuring that was probably as good as it was going to get. I didn't generally wear a lot of makeup, having been blessed with thick dark lashes that made my light gray eyes naturally pop, which I considered a blessing from above because Lord knew I wasn't one to spend a lot of time on body maintenance.

I dressed in leggings and a soft red sweater and put on fuzzy socks since we'd be home the next couple of hours, and I headed down to get a second cup of coffee so I could finish waking up.

I heard Jack talking in his office and figured Carver had called, so I made a detour through the kitchen to freshen my cup and then headed into the office.

Jack's office was one of my favorite rooms. It was toward the front of the house and the entire far wall was windows so it almost looked like the office was outdoors. The ground was covered with a thick blanket of snow, and the pine branches were heavy with white and hung low. Every once in a while you could hear the snap of a tree branch as it collapsed under the weight.

We didn't typically get a lot of snow, at least snow like this, so it was a nice change of scenery. Though after a couple of days when the new had worn off I'd be griping about sunshine and warmer temperatures.

There was a fire blazing in the corner, and Jack sat behind his desk with his socked feet propped up on the edge.

"She just walked in," Jack said, waggling his brows at me.

"Good morning, sunshine," Carver said. "How's my favorite coroner?"

"On my second cup of coffee," I told him.

"We all get to live another day," he said. "Glory be."

Jack snickered and I rolled my eyes, curling up in the overstuffed soft leather chair in the corner.

"You sound unusually chipper for this time of morning," I said.

"That's because this ridiculous snow has us all trapped indoors for the time being, and the baby was up all night with colic, and the toddler stuffed toilet paper in the sink and flooded the bathroom. I haven't even bothered to check on the older two because I'm too afraid of what I'll find. I just toss animal crackers at them randomly and make sure something stimulating is on the television at all times."

"What do you consider stimulating?" Jack asked.

"Action movies," Carver said. *The Fast and the Furious, Lethal Weapon, Bad Boys*...you know, the classics. Though our oldest got a red card from preschool because of inappropriate language. She picked up a couple of catchphrases that aren't received well in polite company."

I was laughing so hard my coffee was threatening to slosh over the edge. "I've got to hand it to you, Carver," I said between giggles. "No one is a better advertisement for birth control than you are. At this rate Jack and I will never have children."

"Just forget the stories I told you about the flooded bathroom and the colic," he said. "Kids are a blessing. I swear. Michelle wanted four kids, and I live to please my wife. You do not want that woman mad."

"Since you're obviously holed up in your office and trying to stall so you don't have to go deal with the flooded bathroom," Jack said, "why don't you tell us what you've got."

"I don't like being that transparent," Carver said, his sigh loud through the speaker. "I'm a trained law enforcement officer."

"Tell that to your bathroom," Jack said.

"That's just mean," Carver said. "But fine. I did the search you asked on one Blake Steed. What kind of stupid name is that anyway? Unless you're in adult films. Then it's probably pretty awesome."

"Focus," Jack said.

"Right," Carver said. "Anyway, maybe Blake always wanted a stage name because up until the age of eighteen, he was known as Travis Hooker."

"Huh," I said. "I can't really say that's a lot better. Why the name change?"

"I'd change my name too," Carver said. "You totally called it, Jack. The kid has a heck of a juvie record. Looks like Mom died when he was six, and then he was raised by an alcoholic father. Nearly beat Blake to death a couple of times before he passed out himself, but he was never in the system long. He always ended up back with the dad.

"Blake's apple didn't fall far from the tree because he was already having trouble with the law by the time he turned twelve—theft, auto theft, destruction of property, underage drinking. Then he hit thirteen and he started to notice girls.

"Over the next two years he got multiple complaints from girls at school or from around his neighborhood saying he sexually assaulted them, but Blake's dad always disputed the charges and gave him an alibi, so nothing ever came of it. Then when Blake was fifteen, a thirteen-year-old girl who lived next door to him was found down the street behind a dumpster. She'd been beaten and raped and strangled, but her attacker didn't realize she wasn't as dead as he thought she was. There was no DNA present, and the girl ended up with permanent brain damage because she went so long without oxygen to the brain. She was never able to name her attacker, but police reports show they looked at Blake hard and believed it was him. But they could tie no evidence to him.

"Then the summer he turned sixteen his father died. Old man drank himself to death. Blake had no living relatives or anyone who could act as guardian, so he took off and lived on the streets. At least for a short time. I guess he'd developed a taste for what he'd started with the girl who lived next door, because he did it again. He got work as a busboy at a restaurant and took an interest in a young woman who came in regularly. Evelyn Bristow. She was a law student at Georgetown. Young and pretty. Everyone liked her. And Blake is a big guy. His pictures show him a little thinner through the shoulders than he is now, but he certainly didn't look sixteen.

"She always walked back to her apartment from the restaurant, and he followed her one night. It's not a bad neighborhood. Pretty good amount of traffic and the neighbors watch out for each other. But Evelyn wasn't so lucky that night. A witness says he saw Blake run up to her and hand her something, like she'd dropped it and he was just being gentlemanly. Since Blake and Evelyn knew each other and they were talking friendly, the witness went about his business and didn't think anything of it until Evelyn's body was found the next morning, behind a dumpster.

"Evelyn was on the small side, but she got a swipe or two in. They found DNA under her nails. She'd been raped, sodomized, and strangled. It was an almost identical crime scene as the other girl."

"And why is he a free man with a new identity now?" Jack asked.

"Ahh, the system at work," Carver said. "He went into the juvie system as a registered sex offender. Got his GED and started college classes. Turns out he's brilliant. He became a real upstanding citizen. Even got a job and went to his mandatory counseling like clockwork. When he turned eighteen, he was considered completely rehabilitated. An exemplary product of a system that works. And some whack-job judge decided it was unfair to label a brilliant young man with such promise as a sexual predator. So he had his juvenile record sealed and gave him a clean slate to start out adulthood. No court reported continuation of therapy or parole. Travis Hooker never existed, and he chose a new name and identity and enrolled in college. And now here he is, dropped in your lap."

"I should have hit him harder," I said, nausea roiling in my stomach. It made me sick to have a monster like that in my presence and not have sensed it until it was almost too late. "Is there any reversal on the ruling if he breaks the law again?"

"No," Carver said. "Once he was cleared, that was it. And his juvie record was sealed. Not to me of course. I've never met a seal I can't break."

"And we're all glad for it," Jack said. "Because it's

going to be my greatest pleasure to see this kid behind bars where he belongs. I'm about to make his life miserable."

"That's the Jack I know and love," Carver said. "Now tell me what's going on with the death of Kaal Dracarian. The message boards are going crazy."

"Seriously?" I asked. "Is he famous or something?"

"Sometimes it's embarrassing to have y'all as friends," Carver said. "Live action RPGs are very popular."

"Role-playing games," Jack said for my benefit, giving me a cocky smile. "I've already been schooled."

"Kaal Dracarian is undefeated," Carver said. "He's basically a god among men. No one has even come close to claiming his territory or his woman."

"Wow," I said, eyes wide. "There's a lot at stake. For people who don't actually exist."

"But in this world, all of these people very much exist," Carver said. "The KGU Kings are a hell of an organization. The whole D&D club is. It's a great farm club for the big leagues. And these guys are brilliant. I wouldn't mind hiring any one of them, but they'd probably make more money in the private sector."

"You keep up with brilliant college kids?" I asked.

"Not all of them," Carver said. "But I created the message boards and forums they use to play games online. It's a program I developed to help track potential hackers and people with exceptional skills. It's how I caught Doug hacking into the US Treasury when he was twelve. Of course, if I'd started the message boards sooner, I would have caught him breaking into the Pentagon a couple of years before."

"*You* were the one who caught Doug and turned him in?" I asked.

"Of course," Carver said. "I can't have him ruining my security clearance. We share a last name. Him getting caught was the only thing that would put him on the straight and narrow. Doug has a criminal side, so he needed some steering in the right direction. And now look at him. I've got my eye on him and he's been allowed to help with the occasional case under strict supervision."

"Speaking of Doug," Jack said. "I've got the sword here at the house. I'd prefer to keep him isolated in case he electrocutes or blows up any innocent bystanders."

"I ran the probability on it," Carver said. "But Doug can confirm. You're probably looking at something as simple as an amped-up cattle prod. Kaal Dracarian wears a full metal chain mail shirt, and he's got metal plates strategically placed on his shoulders and chest. The current probably got trapped inside the metal and ping-ponged around for a while until it was able to find an outlet."

"Would any of those kids know that would happen?" Jack asked.

"All of them would," Carver said. "That's pretty

basic science. And all of them would be familiar with Kaal Dracarian's uniform. He's known worldwide."

"We're heading to go talk to all these kids," Jack said. "Dwight Parr said he didn't make the magnifications to the sword. Which means someone else did."

"Dwight Parr," Carver said. "Talk about brilliant. He won the Archimedes Fellowship. If he murdered your victim his entire life is over. I'd put him on suicide watch, especially if you make an official arrest. If a kid like that can't achieve his dreams, he won't see much purpose in living."

"Good to know," Jack said.

"Oh, and take Doug with you to talk to the other kids. He'll be able to translate the nerd speak."

"You want us to take Doug out in public?" I asked.

"Just do what I do," Carver said. "Feed him every half hour or so and wear earplugs."

CHAPTER SEVEN

JACK LEFT IN HIS TAHOE TO DRIVE THE ROADS AND make sure they were safe before everything opened back up again. The snow had already started to slow in its intensity, and if the sun came out and warmed things up that would be the end of our snow day.

A deputy showed up while Jack was gone to take my statement regarding Blake Steed. Fortunately, it was Durrant and we were on friendly terms after having worked a few cases together.

Durrant was tall and skinny and he had the long narrow face of a poet and puppy-dog-brown eyes that made people underestimate him. His dark hair was always a little unkempt and hung over his forehead.

"Sorry about this, Doc," he said, following me into the kitchen. "Sounds like the guy is a real creep."

"He's a creep all right," I said. "I just want to get

this over with and get a formal complaint on file. I don't want the university trying to pawn him off on someone else. I tried calling the dean of the pathology department, but I haven't gotten a call back. Jack just told me to wait and see if he can dig up any other complaints on Blake. People need to know he's a predator."

"Oh, don't worry," Durrant said. "We're going to make life harder on him. Between you and Miss Emmy Lu's witness statement, the university won't be able to ignore this. I'd be very surprised if this was his first time."

I felt better after talking with Durrant, and it was good to get the complaint filed. Jack still hadn't returned by the time I let Durrant out, so I locked the door behind him and headed to the office to start on the murder board.

I was a visual person, so seeing the crime scene unfold in images and timelines helped in solving cases. Of course, my background was on the human anatomy side of things, so I needed all the help I could get when it came to police procedure. They didn't teach that in medical school.

Jack's office had the best technology money could buy, including a computerized whiteboard that Carver had helped design that couldn't even be bought in a store yet. Despite the joy that simple pleasures like modern technology brought me, I wasn't looking forward to starting Kevin Schwartzman's board. I didn't have a lot of confidence that we'd be able to bring proper justice to Kevin. We were out of our league, and there were so many variables to the murder weapon and the crime scene, it was a very good possibility that a good defense attorney would chew this case up and spit it out. We had to tie this one up tight and put a bow on it.

But at the center of it all, was always the victim. I put a digital photograph of Kevin Schwartzman in the middle of the board, and then I placed some of the autopsy photos and the official report around him. It was always important to remember who we were working for and why.

I saw Jack had already started running background checks on the six remaining members of the Kings level of the D&D club. Their student ID photos popped onto the screen, while the computer searched for everything from parking tickets to arrests. I also put Trish Johnson on the board since she had direct contact with all of the students as the academic sponsor.

I scrolled through her credentials with interest. I'd have placed her in her late twenties or early thirties by appearance, but she'd be forty-five next month. I needed to ask what skin care she was using. She had a PhD in history, and had been teaching American history at the college for three years.

And then my eyes widened in surprise. She also had a PhD in mechanical engineering and had taught in that area of study for the eight years prior to teaching history. That was a nugget of information that hadn't come out when we'd talked with her. But it would certainly explain her interest in the live role-play D&D club, considering almost all of the upper-level students came from the engineering department.

Just for kicks I put Jim Coleman on the board, mostly because he'd rubbed me the wrong way and I wanted to be nosy about the kind of people who were trying to butter Jack up. But other than wanting to lawyer up so fast, he was pretty far down on the suspect list. As the president of the university, he didn't have much day-to-day interaction with the students.

I went through the evidence folder and put the picture that had been found in Kevin's wallet up on the board. The photograph was one of the small black-and-whites that were printed from a photo booth. I was going to have to disagree with Jack on this one. This girl didn't seem like a relative. Kevin looked like he was head over heels in love, and though the girl was smiling, she didn't have the same gleam in her eyes, even though her body was leaning slightly toward him.

I looked at the pictures of the two girls in the Kings division—Miley George and Savannah Rowe—but neither of them were the girl in the photo with Kevin. We needed to find that girl.

Even as I had the thought, I heard the front door open and close with a great deal of fanfare and laughter.

"Doug," I whispered, and headed out of the office.

Doug Carver was the spitting image of his uncle, only he hadn't quite stopped growing yet. He was over six feet tall and reed thin, with shaggy blond hair that constantly hung down in his eyes. He was wearing a black hoodie with a skull on the sleeve and the hood was pulled up over his head.

"It's freezing outside," I said. "How are you in shorts?"

"I'm hot blooded," he said, waggling his eyebrows. "How's it going, Doc? Ready to leave this guy?"

"Nah, he keeps me well fed and I like his pillows," I said. "I'll keep him around."

"Your loss," he said, giving me a lopsided grin identical to his uncle's.

"Maybe you could help me with these bags instead of flirting with my wife," Jack said.

"Oh, I was hoping you'd be done with that by now," Doug said, giving Jack the same grin, but hefting two of the duffle bags.

"Are you moving in?" I asked, slightly panicked at the sight of a large suitcase, two duffle bags, and a carry-on.

"The duffle bags have all my snacks," he said. "Sometimes you guys run out, and you don't have delivery here so it takes forever to get replacements when I run out of food. You know I have to eat constantly. Otherwise I get sick, and you don't want that. I'm a projectile vomiter."

"Awesome," I said, looking at Jack. "Maybe we should put him out in the shed."

"He'd just eat the deer feed we keep stored out there," Jack said.

"Man, I can't believe Kaal Dracarian was murdered," Doug said, immediately heading into the kitchen and dropping the duffle bags on the breakfast table. "That's, like, crazy, man. Anyone who knows Kaal knows he's got something special going. It's just a cheap shot to take out the best player in the game. Where's the challenge in that?"

Jack's ears perked up at that. "You think someone could have killed Kevin because they wanted to knock him out of his spot?"

"Sure," Doug said. "It's the only reason I can think of. Kaal Dracarian is the highest-ranked player in the entire university league. He gets his full tuition paid for as long as he claims the top spot."

"You're joking," I said. "They give scholarships for games like this?"

"They give scholarships for everything now," Doug said, going over to the fridge and sticking his head inside. "E-sports and live role-play are real athletic events, and schools pay big bucks to get the best kids in the nation on their team. There's competitions all over the world."

"Athletic events?" Jack asked amazed.

"We're a new generation of athletes," Doug said, coming out of the fridge with a stack of sandwich meat and cheeses to make a sandwich.

"I can see that," Jack said dryly. "Jaye and I have to run to campus and talk to some kids this morning."

"I'll go with you," Doug said. "You might need a translator. I'll make this sandwich to go, and put my bags in my room."

He made several sandwiches and stuck one in his mouth, and then grabbed his duffle bags and headed out of the kitchen. He was back in a matter of moments and the sandwich was gone.

"I'd like to make a couple of suggestions for my room," he said, grabbing the extra sandwiches off the counter and shoving them in the pocket of his hoodie. "No offense, but it's kind of plain. What's up with all the neutrals? Have you become the Chip and Joanna Gaines of Virginia?"

"Wow, those two really reach a wide demographic," I said.

"My mom has all their books lying out all over the place," Doug said. "She's hopeless when it comes to home renovation stuff. She tried to shiplap our living room, and it's tilted all kinds of ways so it's like walking into a fun house and you lose your balance. I kind of like it better that way.

"Anyway," he said, pausing to take a breath. "I was thinking we could paint a couple of walls a color. Like black. And maybe we could put some mirrors and posters on the walls."

"I'm going to go with no on the black paint," Jack said. "It's a guest room and you're a guest. Not a permanent resident."

Doug cleared his throat and made his way toward the front door. "Well, in case you wanted to make me a permanent resident my mom said it was okay. She says I need a man's influence so I don't end up in jail."

"What about your Uncle Ben?" Jack asked, stopping at the door with his hand on the knob.

"Mom says Uncle Ben has enough to deal with right now, and that it's not fair to Michelle to have two Carvers under the same roof."

"Fair enough," Jack said, making eye contact with me. "Let's revisit this conversation again later."

I wasn't sure what had just happened, but there had been a vulnerability in Doug's voice that normally wasn't there, and I wondered if more was going on at home than Carver had let on. All we really knew was that Doug lived with his single mother, who happened to be Ben's sister. She lived in Virginia, so she wasn't far, but I had no idea what she did for a living or how she managed to parent a kid like Doug. He'd broken into the Pentagon at the age of nine and the United States Treasury at twelve. There weren't a lot of after-school programs for kids like that.

But Carver had saved Doug's bacon and gotten him on the straight and narrow. He'd recently turned sixteen and he'd started college last fall. He might be in college, but he was still a very young teenager, which made him like a fish out of water on campus. I had to imagine it was hard for a kid as smart as Doug to fit in anywhere. And maybe his mom figured she was limited in what she could do for him.

Jack set the alarm and locked the door and we headed to the Tahoe.

"Aww, man," Doug said. "You know I have PTSD sitting in the back of police units, eyeing the back door."

"That's good," Jack said. "That means you learned your lesson. And if it makes you feel better, there are perks to being the sheriff. No naked behinds or vomiting drunks have sat in this hallowed space. In fact, I think you might be the only person I've transported in all my time as sheriff."

"I guess that makes me feel a little better," Doug said, getting into the back seat and reaching in his pocket for a sandwich."

"You'd better pace yourself," I said. "It might be a couple of hours before we get back home."

"That's the great thing about college campuses," he said. "Food everywhere. Who are we going to talk to?"

"It's the on-campus LARP group," Jack said.

"Nice," Doug said. "Look at you learning your vocab."

"Help me out," I said.

"Live action role-play," Jack and Doug said together.

"It's the D&D club," Jack continued. "But we're specifically talking with the Kings."

"Shut the front door," Doug said.

For a moment, I thought maybe he'd choked on his sandwich because Doug was never quiet that long.

"We're going to see the Kings?" he finally asked. "They're, like, legend."

"I bet you're smarter than all of those guys," I said. "How come you're not competing against them?"

"I'm not allowed to do online gaming of any kind," he said. "It was part of my release program Uncle Ben set up. The higher-ups think that video games lead to criminal activity or something stupid like that."

"Ahh," I said. "Sorry."

"No worries," he said. "I still have all my game systems, and I keep up to date with all the major players. They only said I couldn't play. They never said I couldn't watch."

"Loopholes everywhere," I said, the corner of my mouth twitching.

It was a twenty-minute drive to KGU, so I took the time to tell Jack what I'd discovered when I'd started the murder board.

"I think we need to talk to Trish Johnson again," I said. "Up until three years ago, she was a professor in the engineering department. It seems to me she might have the know-how to do something like that to a sword too. And she certainly didn't volunteer that information. She'd have known Kevin and any of the other seniors or grad students from her time in that department."

"Isn't she teaching history now?" Jack asked. "That seems like a pretty drastic switch to go from engineering to history."

"And super boring," Doug added.

"She's got PhDs in both," I said. "Maybe she thought it was time for a switch."

"It's definitely a question worth asking," he said. "We're supposed to meet the Kings in Jubilee Hall. It's where they have their club meetings."

"Righteous," Doug said. "You guys don't even understand how lucky you are right now. Most of these people are never seen out of costume or offline. It's like they're living underground or something. No one uses their real names. It's what makes their characters come to life. They're probably going to be pretty pissed to see you."

"That ought to make things more interesting," Jack said, parking the Tahoe in front of Jubilee Hall.

One of the perks of riding in a police unit was that you could park anywhere you wanted to, and one I'd miss if Jack ever decided to hang up the uniform.

I'd remembered my scarf and gloves this time, and I was bundled up in my black down coat with the fur hood and my weatherproof boots. The problem with winter is that being bundled up feels great for the short time you're outside, but the second you walk indoors it's like walking into an oven.

Jack opened one of the double doors that led into Jubilee Hall and I walked in first, immediately yanking at my scarf and pulling off my gloves. I unzipped the coat, and noticed Jack and Doug were doing the same thing. There was a coatrack just inside the door and we all hung our things there.

"I guess they'll still be there when we get back," I said.

"I'm sure it'll be fine," Jack said.

"You sure are trusting for a cop," I said, making Doug snicker.

The entryway smelled of must and old wall paneling, and it was obvious it was one of the older classroom buildings on campus. Large ornate frames hung on the wall, of old men who'd either donated a lot of money to the university or were one of the founders.

"Do you have a portrait hanging in one of these halls?" I whispered to Jack.

He pressed his lips together, and didn't answer.

"You do," I accused. "I want to see it? Where is it? Are you dressed like the guys in these paintings?"

"You'll have to scour every hall on campus to find it," he said. "All I can say is that my father made me do it. And I'll leave it at that."

I was going to get in a couple more jabs about the portrait, but Trish Johnson came down the marble stairs to our right. She was dressed more professionally today, in black slacks and a dark gray sweater that showed off her figure better than the clothes she'd had on the day before. She wore her hair down today, and it curled in layers to the middle of her back. I noticed she also wore makeup, and the added enhancements changed her from a very pretty woman to drop-dead gorgeous.

"Holy smokes," Doug whispered. "I want to transfer here."

I smacked him lightly on the back of the head so he'd close his gaping mouth. "You've got some drool on your chin."

CHAPTER EIGHT

"Sheriff Lawson," she said, moving forward to shake Jack's hand. "Dr. Graves." She nodded in my direction. "I wanted to meet you down here before you talk to the students. They're really having a difficult time with Kevin's death. They were all very close. More like siblings than friends."

"I understand," Jack said. "But like you said, they knew Kevin better than anyone. And they know each other better than anyone. Someone in that room will know something about the magnifications made to that sword."

She nodded, but I could tell she was annoyed that he was going to infiltrate their secret society. "I'm sorry," she said, looking at Doug. "But this is a private area and no other students are allowed to enter."

"He's not a student here," Jack said. "He's actually being loaned to us from the FBI. He's something of a wunderkind with this sort of thing. So he'll be coming with us."

"The FBI hires teenagers?" she asked, skeptically.

"They do when they're as brilliant as he is," Jack said. "Since I have you alone, I'd like to ask you about your transfer to the history department three years ago."

Trish froze, and she stared at Jack with eyes that gave nothing away. "What would you like to know?"

"Why did you move from the engineering department to history?" he asked.

"I was ready for a change of pace," she said. "The engineering department is very competitive. There's always new research and papers and articles that have to be published. I also have a fondness for history, so I decided to make the transfer. It gives me more time to have a life outside of the science building."

"Did you ever teach Kevin when you were in engineering?"

"Sure," she said. "I taught almost all of the upper classmen in the Kings. I taught a freshman intro class."

"Why didn't you mention that when we spoke yesterday?"

"I didn't think it was relevant," she said.

"You didn't think it relevant to mention that you possess the skills to enhance the sword that killed Kevin Schwartzman?"

She laughed, but there wasn't humor in it. "I'm

an optical engineer, not mechanical or electrical. I don't have the skill to do anything with that sword but swing it at an opponent. You can follow me and I'll take you to where we're meeting."

Trish didn't wait for Jack to ask any more questions, and I looked at Jack to see if he was going to let her get away with it or make her come back just to put her in her place. But he subtly shook his head at me and told me to follow.

There was no point pressing her too soon. I knew how Jack worked. Whatever she'd said had been enough to pique his interest and cause him to start digging deeper.

I was the first to follow Trish up the stairs, so I got the full effect of her hips in motion. I heard Doug trip behind me and figured he'd gotten a glimpse as well.

Trish led us up three flights of stairs, and I was slightly winded by the time I got to the top. I wasn't one of those people who enjoyed cardio, unless sex was involved, so this was as good as a complete workout for the day.

Once we got to the top of the third-floor landing, she led us into a large room that looked like the library had rejected it. There were rows and rows of bookshelves, but none of the books were ordered and there were no sections that I could see. The smell of dust and old pages made Doug sneeze as we were led down the middle row toward a glassed room that looked similar to a DJ booth in a radio station.

"This is where the broadcast team started before they were moved to the new building," Trish said before I could ask.

I wasn't sure if the team was given this location because it was hard to find, or because it was the only thing left available on campus, but it didn't seem like an ideal spot to host a group. We took another turn and there was a large red door with chipped paint on the frame and an exit sign above. She opened it and it led us into a stairwell that only went up.

"I guess this is how you stay in shape," I said, trying not to sound too winded as I spoke. I noticed Jack was having no trouble at all, but it made me feel a little better to see Doug red faced and huffing.

Trish smiled. "Half of these kids are asthmatics and I'm convinced the other half have never stepped foot outdoors. It just goes to show how bad they want to be here that they make this trek to do what they love."

"How often does the group meet?" Jack asked.

"Officially, they meet twice a week, Tuesday and Friday from six to ten in the evening," she said. "Unofficially, they meet almost every night of the week. No one else has this space booked."

"I can't imagine why," Doug said, bending at the waist and taking deep breaths.

"Here we go," she said as we came to another red door like the last one.

There was also an exit sign above this one, and I

had to wonder where exactly people were exiting to in case of an emergency.

Trish had a key ring in her hand with a single brass key on it.

"Seems like a lot of precautions for something as simple as an extracurricular campus activity," Jack said.

"I'm sure it seems that way, but there's a lot at stake here," she said.

"Like full tuition for the number one ranked player?" Jack asked.

"That's certainly a big part of it," she said. "Each tournament also has cash prizes. You have to understand that even though the Kings are a team and they run scenarios and strategies by each other, they all keep things close to the vest. This is an individual sport."

Trish led us into a heavily air-conditioned room that was pitch black. I grabbed on to the back of Jack's shirt and we shuffled forward until Trish pulled back a black curtain.

"It's the old black box theater," she said. "There used to be a main entrance from the front of the building but they sealed it off when they did renovations."

The room was a mess. There were props and chairs and drop cloths scattered all over the place. We walked down the aisle to the first row, and the five college-aged kids that had been in deep discussion went silent and stared at us with varying levels of curiosity and animosity. I recognized all of their faces from the student ID photos I'd put on our murder board earlier. There were two missing—Kevin Schwartzman and Dwight Parr.

"Hey guys," Trish said. "This is Sheriff Lawson and Dr. Graves that I told you about. They want to find out exactly what happened to Kevin as much as we do. Talk to them and tell them what you know. Anything, no matter how small, could help."

"Thanks," Jack said, nodding at Trish. "I'd like to get all of your legal names for the record."

"Wait a second," one of the guys said. "Who's the kid?"

"He's one of the experts in this particular area that the FBI loaned out to us," Jack said. "Think of him as a translator."

"Some of our information is proprietary," the same guy said. "And he looks like a gamer."

"He's prohibited from competing or taking part in anything that has to do with investigations," Jack assured him. "Why don't we start with you. What's your name?"

"Dagger," the kid said.

"The name your parents gave you," Jack said patiently.

"Nikhil Noriega."

Nikhil was dark skinned and on the small side, maybe a few inches over five feet, and he had black eyes and the kind of lashes women would kill for. His dark hair was shaved on the sides and he wore the rest of it up in a man bun on top of his head.

"Were you and Kevin close?" Jack asked.

"We're family here," Nikhil said. "As you can see, there aren't many who are at our level. We don't really socialize outside this room."

"Kevin did," the girl next to Nikhil said.

"Shut up, Psy," Nikhil said. "Just because Kevin never looked twice your way doesn't mean you have to be a bitch now."

I watched the girl go pale with anger. She was mixed race and freckles covered the bridge of her nose and cheeks, and she had a small ring in one nostril. Her hair was turquoise and cut short and spiky, and she wore a thick layer of eyeliner. So maybe they weren't as much of a family as they pretended to be.

"What's your name?" Jack asked the girl.

"Miley," she said. "Miley George. But everyone calls me Psypher."

"Kevin didn't spend as much time with the group as the rest of you do?" he asked.

She shrugged and looked resentful. "He used to. He was about to graduate. Other things were coming up. Uridak was the same way, especially since he won that fellowship."

"Lord Uridak?" Jack asked. "Dwight Parr?"

"Yeah," the guy next to Miley said. "I'm Jaden Matthews, by the way. Also known as Thunderclap."

His grin was cocky and very un-nerd-like, but the rest of him hadn't caught up yet. He had bright red hair that he'd slicked back with gel, and he had legs longer than Jack's. He looked to be older than

Nikhil and Miley.

"I've been around a while, so I've seen the cycle," Jaden said, and then he explained. "I'm a grad student. Things get busy senior year. I decided to do my graduate work here just so I could continue with the Kings. I didn't want to give any momentum to another school I've been rivals with the last few years."

"Were Kevin and Dwight looking at doing something like that?" I asked. "Switching to a rival school?"

"I don't know," Jaden said. "All Dwight has been able to talk about is Oxford. I think once he won the fellowship, he kind of checked out of the things going on here."

"Did Dwight ever win at any of the tournaments?" Jack asked. "Any of the cash prizes?"

"Sure, all the time," Jaden said. "I mean, he's ranked second next to Kaal. I mean Kevin."

"So with Kevin gone, Dwight moves to the top of the list for tuition," Jack said.

Jaden must have realized that gave Dwight a pretty good motive for killing Kevin, so he hurried to say, "Yeah, but the Archimedes Fellowship covers his tuition anyway."

"Only for the three-month summer program," the girl who'd been quiet up to this point said. "And before you ask, I'm Midnight. But my real name is Savannah Rowe."

Savannah was dressed in black from her

combat boots to the black skullcap pulled down over white-blond hair that came to her shoulders.

"Geez, Mid," Nikhil said. "What's with you and Psy? Why are you trying to throw people under the bus?"

"All I'm saying is that Kaal is dead, and we all saw who killed him. Why would you try to defend Uridak after that?" She dashed a tear from her eye, and pulled her legs up in the chair, wrapping her arms around her knees.

"So if Dwight was in the top player position, it would cover his tuition when he started grad school in the fall?" I asked.

"Not really," Jaden jumped back in. "Only if he was going to grad school in the United States. And only if he was going to a school that participated in the league. Different countries have their own requirements. The World Championship is played every June, and the winner of that gets a hundred-thousand-dollar cash prize."

"So essentially at the end of this semester," Jack said, "The current top two players are no longer a threat."

"Exactly," Jaden said, beaming at us like we were prize students.

"Where can we get a list of the player ranks?" Jack asked.

"It's all online on the main website," Trish said. "But I can give you a list of all of the students who are enrolled in the LARP League from KGU."

"That would be helpful," Jack said. "And what about you? You've been awfully quiet."

He was speaking to the last young man in the group. I recognized him from my murder board, but the picture must have been old because he looked older and mostly...normal.

"David Englander," he said. "They call me Leonidas."

David looked like a fish out of water. Or like he belonged on the football field instead of in this dark theater. He wore jeans and a KGU sweatshirt and faded tennis shoes. His dark hair was cut and well kept, and he didn't have any tattoos or piercings. He was also built like a man—with broad shoulders and a physique that was obvious under his sweatshirt.

"Are you a graduate student?" Jack asked.

"I'm a junior," he said. "But I was delayed a couple of years. I joined the National Guard out of high school, so it was two years before I could start college full time. I'm still in the reserves so I get called out occasionally."

"What was your impression of Dwight and Kevin? Any bad blood between them?"

"Not really," he said. "They were competitive. We all are. But when it was time to hang out or run scenarios, they were the guys everyone listened to. They're both geniuses."

Nikhil scoffed. "Everyone here is a genius."

"Kevin was better at strategy than anyone," David said. "And you know it. He helped you defeat the Night Watchman in round one yesterday. And he's helped us all improve our online tactics."

"What about the sword Dwight used?" Jack asked.

Nikhil and Jaden broke into huge grins, and even Miley's face lit with excitement.

"Can you believe that thing?" Nikhil asked.

"Wicked," Jaden said. "Completely wicked."

"Also a murder weapon," Savannah said angrily. "It killed Kaal."

Jack turned his attention to her. "How do y'all normally go about enhancing your weapons?"

"We each tweak a little here and there," she said. "We're all in the engineering or physics department, so it's trial and error. We come up with new ideas and take apart spare electronics and put them back together again, and then we apply it and see if it works."

"Was that the same for Dwight's sword?" Jack asked.

"Up until yesterday," Savannah said. "None of us have ever seen anything like that. He'd obviously been keeping it to himself to reveal."

"That Archimedes Fellowship went to his head," Nikhil said, his jealousy obvious. "Ever since he got it, he stopped showing us his progress."

"That's not true," David said. "He shared as much as we all do. We never tell each other everything we have planned for the exact scenario that happened yesterday."

"What scenario?" I asked.

"It's a random drawing in tournaments of who fights against each other," David said. "Thunderclap and Midnight drew each other in the first round."

"I won," Jaden said.

"And Kaal is still dead," Savannah said. "Get over yourself and think of someone else for a change."

"Doesn't matter anyway," Nikhil said. "The whole tournament has been cancelled. All of yesterday's points have been erased and we'll have to make them up at 'a later date,'" he said, giving air quotes.

"Nikhil," Trish said reprovingly, and he pressed his lips together tightly.

Jack opened up his phone and scrolled through it and then handed the phone to Savannah. "Does anyone recognize the girl in that photo?"

The others leaned toward Savannah to get a good look at the picture, and there were a myriad of reactions. Miley looked furious. Jaden and Nikhil snickered. David was as stoic as he'd been through the whole interview, and Savannah wiped at more tears.

"Poor Kevin," Savannah said, finally using his real name. "Life just isn't fair." She passed the phone back to Jack and I saw Doug lean over to take a look. I'd almost forgotten that he was there with us since he hadn't uttered a word.

"Whoa," Doug said, taking the phone out of

Jack's hand for a closer look. "Kevin is the guy in the Loser in Lust video?"

"What?" Jack asked, taking his phone back, but he was looking at the others for their reactions.

"You guys really need to spend more time online," Doug whispered. "The Loser in Lust video was in the top ten of most-viral videos of last year. It's brutal, man."

"The girl in the picture with Kevin is Madison Marbury," Savannah said. "She's the same girl in the video. I don't want to do this anymore. I feel sick."

"We're done for now," Jack said. "I'll be back in touch individually if I have any other questions." Then he looked at Trish and said, "We'll find our way out."

CHAPTER NINE

DOUG HAD US DRIVE-THRU FOR CHEESEBURGERS AND fries since it was well past lunchtime, and if I had to hear that he was starving one more time I couldn't be held accountable for my actions.

"You eating?" Jack asked.

"I'm not turning down a free meal," I said. "Give me a cheeseburger with the works and fries. And a chocolate shake."

Jack shook his head. "I don't know how you fit all that in your body."

"It's my superpower," I said. "You know you want one. Your body can't be a temple every day."

"But will you still love me with a potbelly?" Jack asked.

"Meh," I said, pausing dramatically. "Maybe not now that I think about it. Nothing but rabbit food for you from now on."

"Harsh," Doug said.

"I'm joking," I told him, rolling my eyes. "Seriously, Jack. You know you'll start working and won't eat the rest of the day. Get a cheeseburger. It's real meat. It says so right there on the menu."

"Yeah, but the real meat of what animal?" Jack asked and put in our order.

"If you guys are curious," Doug said, "I looked up the rankings roster while you guys were arguing over food. I told you that KGU had one of the best LARP teams in the country, and the standings speak for themselves. They've got five top ten players."

"Who?" Jack asked, taking a bite of burger.

"Well, we already know Kaal Dracarian and Lord Uridak are in the one and two spots. In the number four spot is Thunderclap. Followed by Leonidas in the five spot and Psypher in the nine spot."

"Who's in the three spot?" I asked.

"Ronin Rodgers," Doug said. "He's out of USC, but nobody likes him. He scores dirty. Doesn't get his points honorably."

"Was he at the tournament yesterday?" I asked.

"Yeah, he actually lost to Leonidas. I was watching it on television and I caught their match. It was a great fight. Leonidas would've been within a couple of points of taking the spot from Thunderclap if the tournament hadn't been cancelled."

"Seriously?" Jack asked. "These things are on TV?"

"Sure, I keep telling you it's a sport. ESPN

covers it just like they do poker and all that other weird stuff."

"So a guy like David joins the military out of high school," I said, "Serves his country, and then starts college on the GI Bill. Which means he's doing this for fun?"

"GI Bill will only cover highest tuition of a state school, and KGU is a private university. So anything above and beyond is up to him to cover."

"Hmm," I said. "Maybe we need to take a closer look at Jaden Matthews. Money is always a motive. Maybe he figures if he can knock off the players in front of him, he can get the scholarship money quicker."

"We're going to take a closer look at all of them, including Trish Johnson," Jack said. "She was hiding something when we asked her why she decided to move to the history department. There's something there."

Jack turned onto Anne Boleyn and drove down a street filled with craftsman cottages and manicured lawns before the road turned into a two-lane graveled road. There was nothing but trees and land the closer we got to Heresy Road. I'd lived with my parents on that road in a big rambling Victorian that they'd let run down after their interests had turned to the criminal element. They'd funneled most of their money into building a state-of-the-art lab buried underground and burying cash and other valuables in a bunker.

Most of my childhood memories—at least the

good ones—were of Jack and Vaughn and Dickey, my closest friends. My family didn't have normal holidays or birthdays like regular families. Usually my parents decided to take a trip during those times and I was left to be watched by Jack's mom. Little had I known that all of their "trips" were spent smuggling foreign bodies and the contraband inside them to the funeral home.

Jack and I had been married less than a year, but it was only after my father's death that the anxiety had stopped gripping me every time we turned onto Heresy Road. Which was nice considering the house Jack and I shared together was at the opposite end of the long stretch of road.

"I don't understand the whole points thing," I said. "The Kings mentioned earlier about online points. What's the difference between those and the points from the live battles?"

Doug took a giant bite of his second cheeseburger and then began to explain. "So the league is made up of the High Council. They're the ones who oversee the rules and design the quests. Uncle Ben is on the High Council, but don't tell anyone because they're supposed to remain anonymous so they can't be bribed into giving hints to the main quest."

"He told us he designed the message boards," Jack said. "But he didn't mention anything about the High Council."

"It's pretty cool, huh?" Doug asked. "Anyway, the High Council designs the main quest."

"What kind of quest?" I asked.

"It's like a story," he said. "Haven't you ever played Dungeons & Dragons? There's a storyline and you have to do all these tasks and puzzles and riddles and that kind of stuff to move to the next part of the quest. Usually the goal is to rescue a damsel in distress or find buried treasure. Stuff like that. So you do the main quest online and whoever completes them the fastest gets the highest amount of points. And you have to complete all the tasks in each segment of the quest before you can compete in each live tournament. If you don't finish your tasks, you're out of the running completely until the next year.

"It's cool to see all the characters in person you've been playing online," he continued. "The tournaments are a way for each character to stake their claim and protect their homelands. The further you progress in the tournament, the more points you get toward your overall rank. Each of the lesser tournaments usually have a cash or electronics prize. And then you start again with the next segment of the online quest until the next tournament. Kaal Dracarian has been the champion three years running."

"That's incredibly involved and time consuming," I said. "How does Carver have time to do all that?"

"Because he doesn't sleep much," Doug said. "And he makes mad cash. You don't think he supports the whole fam and my mom on an FBI salary do you? That's a joke."

I pressed my lips together tightly to keep from smiling. I guess I'd never thought much about Carver's financial situation. He and Michelle and their four kids lived in a very nice house in DC. But I always assumed it was Michelle's job as an attorney that put them on that level.

Jack parked the Tahoe in front of the house, and we all jumped out, hurrying to the front door to get out of the cold. The snow had already melted from the sidewalks and driveways, but there was still a good amount covering the grass and trees.

"Doug," Jack said. "You're here to take a look at that sword, but no way I'm letting you do it by yourself just in case something goes wrong. I'm going to call in one of the tech people at the sheriff's office to assist."

"I like the sound of that," Doug said. "I always wanted an assistant."

"Yeah, probably best not to call her that," Jack said. "She'll tie you in a knot and let you starve to death."

"Kinky," Doug said.

Jack rolled his eyes. "You've got time to chill out and relax until she gets here. We're going to get some work done in the office."

"Sweet," Doug said. "I could use a snack. And you know I love your media room. That sound system rattles your teeth. It's awesome."

He headed off toward the kitchen, humming a

tune I'd never heard before and thinking about his stomach. I liked seeing him here, not worrying about school or whatever was going on in that big brain of his that caused him to think he was a burden to his mother.

I turned and saw Jack was staring at me, a half smile on his face.

"What?" I asked.

"I can read you like a book, Dr. Graves," he said.

"A black accent wall can be very dramatic," I said, by way of an answer. "It just takes a little creative vision." And then I walked by him and headed into the office, unsure if I'd just unofficially agreed to let Doug move in with us.

Jack walked in right behind me, and I went to the computer, pulling up all the work I'd done earlier back on the whiteboard.

"That's a good start," Jack said, eyeing the pictures I'd placed there. And then I saw his lips twitch at the sight of Jim Coleman. "Let's see what this viral video is all about."

He did a quick internet search and the video came up immediately, and then he sighed. "I already know I'm going to hate this, whatever it is."

"Yeah, I get that feeling too," I said. "Let's see what we've got."

He hit the switch to dim the lights and projected the video onto the wall, and we took a seat on the couch.

The video started playing and a small bedroom came into focus. I could see a portion of a dorm bed neatly made with a simple blue bedspread on top, but my focus was on the back of the girl's head at the bottom of the screen. I couldn't see much of her, only from the shoulders up, but she sat in a chair with her riotously curly hair pinned on top of her head and a spaghetti strap top.

"Come on, Kev," she said. "Don't be shy. You want me to take more off you've got to do your part. Come on out."

There were a few seconds of silence before a door opened off camera and a rustling sound was heard. Then Kevin came into view.

"Yikes," I said, putting my hand over my mouth.

Kevin was dressed in a gold chest plate and a leather Roman skirt, and he wore a red cape around his shoulders. I was already familiar with Kevin's body, having dissected it the day before, so I felt I could speak fairly when I said that wasn't an outfit just anyone could pull off.

"Good," the girl purred. "I've been waiting for this moment for so long. I told you role-play gets me hot. Now dance for me."

"What?" Kevin squeaked.

"Dance for me and I'll take this off," she said, tugging at the strap of her top. "Why don't I turn some music on?"

She reached for a remote and hit a button and something with a lot of bass came on, as if it was ready for exactly this moment.

"Tell me when it's over," I said. "I can't watch this."

And Kevin started to dance for her as best as a kid who'd spent his college years pretending he was someone else could. It was a horrible sight to see, but he was emboldened by the girl's encouraging words for him to grind harder.

She turned off the music and said, "Very good. You've earned a reward." When the girl stood she completely blocked the view of Kevin, and we were finally able to get a good look at her. I couldn't see her face, but I could tell from the back of her that she was a hundred percent out of Kevin's league.

I could see her full outfit now, and she was wearing a short summer skirt with a slinky tank, and she pulled up the hem of the shirt and tugged it over her head, leaving her topless. And then she sat back in the chair again so Kevin came back into view.

"Like what you see?" she asked.

He couldn't speak. Only nodded his head.

"Want to see more?"

He nodded again.

"Then dance again," she said. "And this time do a striptease for me. I want to see what I'm about to get."

I could see Kevin gulp, and the color drained from his face. But there was no turning back. She hit the button on the remote again and the music started once more.

We watched until Kevin stripped off his tighty-whities and was twirling them in the air with a lot more swagger than when he'd started, and then the door of the room burst open with yells and blood-curdling screams. It was complete chaos as four boys ran into the room, picked up a naked Kevin, and ran out of the room with him on their shoulders.

"Replay that last bit again," Jack said, and I hit the back button on the computer. "Watch the last guy to leave. The big blond in the black T-shirt."

I hit play and watched carefully, looking for whatever it had been that Jack had seen. And then I saw it.

"He winked at the girl," I said.

"Shouldn't be too hard to figure out who any of the people in this video are," Jack said. "I'll put in a call to Jim Coleman. I'm sure this isn't the type of publicity he wanted for the university."

"He's probably thinking the same thing about the murder yesterday," I said. "Poor Jim is having a rough year."

"I think Kevin had a worse year," Jack said.

"Unfortunately true," I said. "I can't imagine how anyone could be this cruel to another human being. There's nothing more on the video?"

"No, that's it," Jack said.

"Tell me what you saw that I missed," I said.

Jack had a gift of being able to see almost every-thing in a room at once in great detail. It was an impressive skill that came in handy at every crime scene we'd ever worked.

"Boy's dorm room," Jack said. "Pretty basic and simple as far as furnishings. I just noticed the one bed instead of bunks, so I figure he's in one of the newer apartment dorms. He had a couple of posters on the walls and condoms on the nightstand table. So he was planning on getting lucky. Family photos tacked to his bulletin board, but other than the tidiness of the room, it looks like a normal place a guy would live."

"They said her name is Madison Marbury," I said.

"Yeah, why don't we go pay her a visit."

CHAPTER TEN

I'D NEVER MET LIEUTENANT RACHEL RYAN. THE IT department worked out of a satellite office in Newcastle, and they didn't typically interact with people.

Now that the fire department had gotten a new station and had moved out of the one on the Towne Square, the renovations had started to expand the sheriff's office to take up the entire building on that side of the block. It was a much-needed renovation that would give more space to the jail and the officers. I'd asked Jack if he planned to move the IT guys into the newly renovated building, but he'd told me it was best to leave them where they were.

King George County didn't have a huge population of people, but it did have a lot of land to cover, so the IT department weren't the only ones to work out of satellite buildings. Jack had deputies set up in small annex buildings all over the county so emergency calls could be responded to as quickly as possible.

"Come on in," Jack said to Lieutenant Ryan.

She was a short, middle-aged woman with salt-and-pepper dark hair that was parted down the middle and framed with bangs. She had a pug-like nose and wore big round glasses, and she was dressed in jeans, combat boots, and a KGSO polo shirt in navy blue. Her gun was hidden under her jacket, and I wanted to mention that it might be safer to leave it in her car so she didn't accidentally use it on Doug.

"We've got y'all set up in the kitchen," Jack told her. "This is Doug." And then Jack whispered, "Try not to kill him. I promise he's good at this stuff." And the harsh lines of her face cracked into what resembled a smile.

Jack introduced me to Ryan and then turned to Doug. "Doug, this is Lieutenant Ryan."

"Sweet," Doug responded, but he was staring intently at the sword. "You should come get a look at this thing."

He was wearing latex gloves and he picked the sword up by the hilt, and before anyone could utter a warning, he hit the switch on the side and the blue electrical current ran up the blade like water and sizzled at the tip.

Doug turned it off and his grin said it all. He was impressed. "You want to take this baby apart?" he asked Lieutenant Ryan.

"Do I ever," she said, clapping her hands and

rubbing them together. "You got a sandwich around this place? I could use something to eat."

"Fridge is mostly stocked, except for the stuff I ate." And then Doug looked at us dismissively. "You might need to make a stop at the grocery store before tonight."

"I guess that's our cue to leave," I said to Jack.

I called and checked in with Emmy Lu on the way to interview Madison Marbury.

"How's it going?" I asked when she answered the phone.

"Well, no one has died, so there's that. I guess that's a good and a bad thing in this line of work."

"Things always slow down after the holidays," I said. "I think the stress of being with family kills a lot of people during November and December. By the time January rolls around, people are too worn out to die. Enjoy the break. Things will pick up again."

"Good to know," she said. "The viewing went well last night, and everything went smoothly with the funeral today."

"You're the best, Emmy Lu," I said, meaning it.

"Don't I know it," she said. "If I could stick to this stupid diet I'd be better than the best. How am I supposed to date a man who owns a donut shop and not gain three hundred pounds? Those are delicious donuts. Every time I walk in there and smell all that sugar I turn into a ravenous beast."

"You just need a different outlet. Be a ravenous

beast with Tom instead of the donuts and the calories will melt away."

"Hmm," she said. "You might be on to something there. The man moves as slow as a turtle. Maybe I can help him pick up the pace a little. Got to go." And she hung up.

"Do I want to know?" Jack asked.

"I don't think so," I said. "But maybe steer clear of the donut shop for a couple of weeks."

Jack smiled and used Bluetooth to call Jim Coleman.

"Jack," Jim said heartily. "How are things going with the investigation? This weather has been a godsend, otherwise we would've been overrun with press today."

"What can you tell us about the video that went viral with Kevin and Madison Marbury last year?" Jack asked.

I could practically hear Jim deflate as he sighed.

"Awful mess," he said. "A lot of negative attention for the university, and we had to have a no-tolerance policy written and add mandatory bullying seminars every semester. The boys were kicked out of their fraternity, and the whole organization was put on probation. The girl insisted she Kevin had been seeing each other and she had no involvement in the prank, even though she was also dating Chad Wheeler."

"Was Chad one of the boys in the video?" Jack asked.

"Yeah," Jim said. "And he backed up Madison's

story that she had nothing to do with the scheme, though I never believed it for a hot minute. I figured Chad was trying to protect his girlfriend. But then I found out Madison and Kevin really were dating at the beginning of this school year, so maybe she was telling the truth. Maybe she and Kevin had something going on all along."

I could tell by the sound of his voice he was perplexed by the idea of that being a possibility.

"Can you send me a list of the names of all the students involved in that fiasco?" Jack asked. "We're heading to talk to Madison Marbury right now."

"Sure," Jim said. "I'll have my secretary send you their student files. The disciplinary action taken against the boys is all in there."

"Appreciate it," Jack said. "One more question."

"Shoot," Jim said.

"Trish Coleman. Why'd she transfer departments three years ago?" Jack asked.

"Well, that one is a little more complicated," Jim said. "There are nondisclosures involved."

"I can get a warrant," Jack said.

"I think you'll have to."

"That makes things more interesting," I said after they'd disconnected.

"Yep," Jack said. "You know it's going to be good when people start talking about nondisclosures and warrants."

"Can't be too bad or she wouldn't still have a job teaching," I said.

Jack turned right and we were on campus.

Again. "It takes an act of God for people to get fired nowadays. Society's idea of, 'not too bad' has definitely shifted on the morality scale over the last few decades."

He drove past the student center and wound his way up and down the hills of the two-lane roads that weaved through campus. We passed the arena, which was still blocked off with barricades and crime scene tape. Jack slowed as the hill steepened and we headed to sorority and fraternity row.

Washington Lake sat at the bottom of the hill and the sun glinted off the icy water. To the left of the lake were six brownstones, each with different Greek letters on their gables. To the right of the lake were another six identical brownstones.

"Girls on the right, boys on the left," Jack said, and he veered the Tahoe to the right side of the lake and the Sigma Chi house.

When we got out of the car, competing music blared from different floors as if they were trying to outdo each other.

"Talk about fancy living," Jack said, eyeing the Colonial monstrosity.

"On Mama and Daddy's dime," I said. "The real world comes soon enough I guess. Do you think Doug and Ryan are going to blow up the house? If it blows up again I say we just move. I don't want to go through any more renovations."

"It's probably a fifty-fifty chance," he said. "Come on, let's see if we can track Madison Marbury down."

Despite the music blasting from the floors above, the lobby gave an appearance of class. It looked like an expensive hotel lobby with dark hardwood floors and scattered rugs in shades of cream and white. The walls were white except for the feature wall behind the greeting counter, which was a cream-colored stone. The light fixtures were gold and there were small groupings of furniture positioned around the enormous lobby. To the right of the room was a café-style bistro with a full coffee bar and stocked glass-front fridge with soft drinks and water inside, and two girls were chatting at a bistro table and holding oversized coffee mugs. They stared at us as we walked to the counter.

A dark-haired, perky young woman gave us a full-wattage smile. "How can I help you? Are you visiting your daughter?"

Jack elbowed me in the ribs before I could make a comment about not being old enough to have a college-aged kid, and he said, "Madison Marbury?"

Her smile dimmed and her expression turned sympathetic. "Oh, sure. You probably heard what happened with her boyfriend. Terrible tragedy. All the girls are just reeling, but Madison is really shaken up. She's up in her room. Almost all classes have been cancelled the rest of the week because of what happened yesterday. I'm Holly, by the way. I'm the house director, so however I can make you comfortable just let me know."

"Thanks," Jack said. "We appreciate the hospitality."

"It's the Sigma Chi way," she said. "Who can I say is calling?" She picked up the phone on the desk and her finger hovered over the numbers."

"Sheriff Lawson," he said, showing her his badge. "Do you have a private room we can go to talk?"

"Uhh," Holly said, eyes widening at the sight of the badge. "Is this about Kevin? Is she in trouble? Do I need to call campus police?"

"That's not necessary," Jack said. "We are the police. We just need to talk to her for a few minutes if you could call her down."

"Sure," she said nervously, and she dialed Madison's room number. Someone must have answered because she said, "Hey, it's Holly. Umm, could you come down here for a minute?" And then she lowered her voice to a whisper. "The police are here to see you."

Holly put down the receiver and looked at us. "She said she'd be down in a minute. She's really having a hard time right now. When one Sigma Chi suffers, we all suffer."

Jack didn't have a response to that so he asked again, "Do you have a private place we can talk?"

"Oh, sure," she said. "Y'all can go in the lounge just past the coffee bar. It's empty right now and those French doors close. I'll put a closed sign on them to keep people out."

"I'd appreciate it," Jack said, but his attention was on the young woman who'd just come down the stairs. "Madison Marbury?"

The two girls at the bistro table had stopped their conversation and were paying close attention to what was going on.

"Yes," Madison said.

She was a very pretty girl with a natural, all-American look. She had the most beautiful curly hair I'd ever seen in several shades of blond that managed to look both untamed and sexy. Grief etched her face and there were dark circles under her eyes.

"I'm Sheriff Lawson and this is the county coroner, Dr. Graves," he said. "Can we ask you a few questions? We can go in the lounge for privacy."

She nodded and we headed past the coffee bar and into the lounge. Jack closed the French doors, and Holly taped a sign to one of the glass panes, and then she gave us a thumbs-up before she disappeared.

This room was more lived in. There was a large-screen television on the wall and built-in bookcases filled with books and games. Three white couches sat in a horseshoe in front of the TV and a red felt pool table was in the back of the room. There were giant beanbag chairs and reading nooks scattered in the corners.

Jack took the couch that faced the door and I took a seat next to him, and Madison sat on the couch directly to our left.

"This is about Kevin?" she asked, her voice shaking.

"Yes," Jack said. "We're looking into different

avenues of who might have been behind his murder."

"I thought Dwight killed him?" she asked, confused.

"We think it's more involved than that," Jack said. "Tell us about your relationship with Kevin."

She blew out a sigh. "It's complicated."

"Most relationships are," he said. "Let me help you out. Did your relationship start before or after the video?"

Her cheeks went scarlet and her fists tightened in her lap. "I guess it depends on how you define relationship. I'm an accounting major, and Kevin was in my Calculus 2 class. I was really struggling, but to him it was as easy as speaking English. I couldn't fail the class because I needed it to graduate, so I asked him to tutor me."

Her fists relaxed in her lap and she put her hands beneath her thighs, and then she smiled sadly. "I'm not sure a girl had ever talked to him before. As soon as I asked him his nose started bleeding and he dropped all his books on the floor. Everyone who saw it laughed, including me, but I really needed the help so I helped him gather his stuff and staunch the bleeding and I asked him again. We agreed to meet in the library after dinner. The problem was I was dating Chad at the time."

"Chad Wheeler?" Jack asked, just for clarification.

"Yes." And then she rolled her eyes. "He's a real jerk, but I didn't realize how much of one at that time. I mean, the guys are always playing pranks and stuff over there, and sometimes it's fun as long as you're not the butt of the joke."

"Did y'all meet at the library?" I asked.

"Yes, but Chad was super jealous," she said. "I kept telling him there was nothing to worry about. That it was the kind of nerdy guy who'd remain a virgin for life, but he didn't believe me. So after we were done at the library one night and leaving, Chad was waiting outside to walk with me back to the Sigma Chi house, and he put on this big macho show trying to intimidate Kevin. But I had to give it to Kevin, it's like some other personality took over and the way he stood and cocked his chin was almost defiant. It was kind of hot."

"I bet Chad didn't like Kevin's response," I said.

She chuckled. "Definitely not. I think if Kevin had cowered Chad would've left things alone. But Chad didn't like for anyone to challenge him, and as scrawny and weak as Kevin is—was—" she said, stumbling over the words, "—he still saw Kevin as something he had to conquer. So that's when he decided to get revenge."

"That seems like a pretty extreme response," Jack said.

"You obviously haven't met Chad," she said. "Extreme is a nice way to put it. Dominating, over-bearing, controlling, abusive...any of those descriptions fit."

"How many people knew about the revenge plan?" Jack asked.

"A bunch of us had gone to Beefcakes after a basketball game—it's a burger place off campus—they have a bar there and we can't drink on campus."

Jack nodded, and she continued.

"Anyway it was me and Jennifer. She's one of my sorority sisters. And Chad and three of his brothers. We all used to hang out a lot since Jennifer and Chad's friend Matt were dating. And Chad was just being Chad, and he'd had a couple of beers, and the way he started talking about Kevin was crazy. You'd have thought Kevin was the hottest and strongest guy on earth, and he was talking about how no one was going to try and steal his woman and all this other stuff."

"But you went along with it?" I asked.

She looked ashamed and dropped her head down. "Yeah, I did. It was just supposed to be a stupid prank. I didn't know it would go viral like that. Believe me, I'd have preferred if it hadn't."

"You told the school that you were unaware of the prank and Chad backed you up," Jack pressed.

"Yeah, probably the only chivalrous thing he's ever done," she said.

"So y'all hatched this plan for you to seduce Kevin and record him," Jack said. "How'd you hide the video camera without him knowing?"

"I hid it in his bookshelf while he was in the bathroom," she said.

"Where did Chad and the others take Kevin after they kidnapped him from the room?"

She winced and her hands were back in her lap, white knuckled again. "They chained him to one of the lampposts by the student center. He was there a while before someone found him and called campus police because it was so late at night."

"What happened between you and Chad after that?" I asked. "How'd you end up with Kevin after all?"

"After Chad's one and only act of chivalry, things were just weird between us," she said. "He kept accusing me of sleeping with Kevin, saying I was way too comfortable stripping for him, like I'd done it a thousand times before. Stuff like that. And then he got disciplined by the school for hazing and he and his friends all got kicked out of the fraternity and he lost his scholarship. Talk about pissed..."

"I can imagine," Jack said. "Pissed enough to want to kill Kevin?"

"Definitely," she said.

"Did he have to quit school?" I asked.

"No, he got a job and student loans to make tuition," she said. "Last I heard he should graduate in May."

"What's Chad's major?" Jack asked.

"Electrical engineering," she said.

CHAPTER ELEVEN

"I'M GOING TO BE HONEST WITH YOU," JACK SAID.
"There's always different sides to a story based on
who was involved and what was witnessed. But
something doesn't ring true here. Help me understand how you went along with a prank like this,
your boyfriend vouched for you, and then you
somehow ended up being the girlfriend of the guy
you screwed over?"

She started to cry then, her shoulders shaking
as she tried to keep her sobs silent. I had to agree
with Jack. It was hard to have any sympathy for her
because as of this moment, she looked like one of
the greatest and most manipulative actresses we'd
ever come across. It's not easy for a person who
participated in something like that to come up
smelling like roses with no consequences, unless
they lied through their teeth and everyone believed
them.

There was a box of Kleenex on the bookshelf

and I got up and grabbed the box, setting it down in front of her.

"Tha...thank you," she managed to say. "I know how I look, and I know you have no reason to believe me. But all I can say is that I'm sorry I participated in the prank. Kevin is—was—a sweet guy. I liked him a lot, even when he was just tutoring me. He is—was—really smart. Like, really smart. It's just that he had this reputation because he lived in this fantasy world with all those other weirdos. But I think he was just afraid to see what the world had to offer outside of the one he made up."

"I think he saw pretty clearly after he was humiliated in front of millions of people," Jack said. "How'd you turn the tide and get Kevin to go out with you?"

"That's the thing, Kevin pursued me," she said. "Chad and I broke up a couple of weeks after the whole thing happened, right at the end of the semester. And I stayed on campus because I was taking summer classes, and it just so happened Kevin was too. I thought he hated me. He never came back to calculus after the video went viral. He got permission to do all his classes online or meeting privately with the professors. It turns out he did hate me."

My brows rose at that bit of information. "What do you mean by that?"

"Things kind of calmed down over the summer, and Kevin started going back to class in person.

The math and engineering department share a building. I was just getting out of class and he was just...there. He acted like nothing had ever happened. Like he was over it, and when I asked him about it, he said he knew I was as used by Chad as he had been and that there were no hard feelings.

"He made me feel good, especially since I'd been feeling so terrible for the past weeks. I thought, yeah, maybe I'd been as much of a victim of Chad as Kevin had been. And then I didn't start to feel so bad."

"So you and Kevin started dating?" Jack asked.

"Yeah," she said. "It just kind of happened. We were spending all our time together and he was telling me about the Kings and the LARP tournaments and that he was ranked number one in the nation and that it's what paid for his tuition. He said that money was a huge help to his family because they hadn't figured out how to cover the rest of his tuition, even though he had a great academic scholarship already. This is a private university, so it's crazy expensive, you know?"

"Yeah," Jack said. "I know. Did he introduce you to his friends?"

She shrugged. "He tried to, but they're a pretty close-knit group. Like I said, weirdos. If you're not in that elite circle they won't have anything to do with you. And Kevin started spending more time with me instead of with the group, and I thought he really liked me. One thing led to another, and then he was sneaking me into his dorm room at night. He's got one of the new apartments so he doesn't have a roommate. Just a suitemate. It's like he was a totally different person. Like he'd really come out of his shell. He told me he couldn't live the role-play life forever, and that he had to figure out what he wanted to do in the real world.

"I thought he loved me. We'd been talking a lot about our futures and our hopes and dreams. I've been offered some internships and things like that, and he was helping me decide what I should do after graduation."

She started crying again, and this time I had a sinking feeling in my gut and I looked at Jack and knew he felt the same.

"Right before Christmas," she said, wiping her nose with the Kleenex. "He sets up a romance dinner at a really nice restaurant in town. He'd worked it out with the restaurant to have a private room with candles and rose petals. The whole nine yards. There was wine and we dressed up, and I thought he was going to propose."

She shrugged, and there was bitterness in her voice. "But he didn't propose. He put the whole dinner together to show me a video he'd made. He pulled out his laptop at the end of dinner and told me he had something for me to watch. Kevin's really talented, so at first I thought it was this amazing proposal video because it was such high quality. But then I realized he'd been recording us every time I stayed the night with him. He must have had cameras all over his dorm room because there wasn't an angle that wasn't seen, and he meshed it all together so it looked like it was...you know...professional. You couldn't ever see his face though. Just mine.

"I just kind of sat there in shock," she said. "That's the only word to describe it. There wasn't even time for me to get mad, because as soon as it was over, he started talking about how revenge was sweet, and he'd enjoyed a different kind of role-playing over the last few months. He said it had taught him a lot. That *I* had taught him a lot. He told me I deserved what I got for how I treated him, and that Chad deserved something even worse.

"Then while I was watching he pulled up this screen on the computer and asked if I knew what it was? But he didn't really want an answer. He was happy to tell me that it was the email addresses of everyone who'd offered me internships and emails for the deans I'd been in talks with for possible grad school. The link for the video had already been uploaded and he attached my resume so they'd know who I was. And then he hit send."

"Did you report it?" Jack asked.

Her eyes blazed at Jack. "To who? The more people I reported it to the more the video would circulate."

"What did you do after he hit send?" I asked.

"Just sat there," she said. "I felt like my heart had stopped beating. I couldn't move. Couldn't function. And Kevin just smiled at me, got up, gave me a kiss on the top of the head, and he left. The waiter brought the check soon after for me to pay, and I had to call someone for a ride home.

"I should have known though," she said. "I don't know why I didn't see it. He practically told me how that stupid Kaal Dracarian conquered every battle he fought. He lured me in and told me what I wanted to hear, all the while collecting all the information he needed to destroy me."

"Did it destroy you?" I asked.

"Well, I have no internships after I graduate and I didn't get into the two graduate schools I applied for, so you tell me. He put it online on several of the porn sites. I'm sure he was making money off of it. Jerk." She wiped furiously at her tears.

"You said he told you that Chad deserved something worse," Jack said. "Did he ever deliver on that?"

"I don't know," she said. "But I texted Chad and let him know that Kevin was gunning for him and to watch out."

"Dang," Jack said once we were back in the car. "I think that tops the top of any revenge story I've ever heard."

"These kids are all kind of awful," I said. "Savannah was the only friend of Kevin's who bothered to shed a tear for him. The others were all like vultures, ripping at his corpse."

"Lovely image," he said. "But I hear what you're saying."

"And then we know Professor Trish is hiding something," I continued. "And now Madison Marbury has a pretty big motive for wanting Kevin dead. Maybe she and Chad teamed up to take care of him once and for all. Electrical engineering."

"Yeah, I'm really interested in what Chad has to say," Jack said. "Why don't we see if he's home?"

But he wasn't home. Chad had been kicked out of the fraternity house so he and the three others involved in the incident had moved off campus and were renting a house a couple of blocks away. It wasn't a great area of town, and the little white house looked like something that four college boys could afford.

There were no cars in the driveway or lights on in the house that we could see, and Jack left me in the car and went to see if anyone answered the door.

When he came back, he said, "I'll have a deputy come by early in the morning and pick him up for questioning at the station."

His phone rang, but I could tell by the look on his face he didn't recognize the number.

"This is Sheriff Lawson," he said, and was silent for a few seconds. "We're actually close to campus now. We can meet you there in five minutes."

He hung up and said, "That was Savannah Rowe. She and Jaden Matthews want to talk to us."

"About what?"

"She didn't say," he said, putting the Tahoe in drive. "She just said they wanted to talk to us. They'll meet us at Campus Coffee."

"Praise the Lord," I said. "I could use a dose of caffeine."

"You're an addict," he said.

"There are much worse addictions," I told him. "Heroin, social media, eating paint chips..."

"Ahh, I'd forgotten about that one," Jack said.

"Hey, I saw some weird stuff in medical school. Coffee is natural. It's a bean. And beans are good for you. Like a salad."

"There's a lot wrong with those statements," Jack said. "But if I ever roll over and you've turned into a mummified husk of a coffee bean, just know that I'll give you the best send-off money can buy, and I'll never drink coffee again in your honor. Unless my new wife likes coffee and then I'll probably have some."

I punched him in the shoulder. "If I die, you're coming with me," I said. "I don't care if I have to drag you screaming into the grave. I remember something in our marriage vows about two becoming one."

He gave me the side-eye and said, "If I died at a young age would you remarry?"

"Of course not," I said. "I've gotten used to you, and I don't really feel like having to break someone else in. But I'll think of you while I spend all your money."

"Good to know," he said. "Here we are."

Campus Coffee was on the corner of University Drive and wasn't actually on the KGU campus, but it was close enough to count. Jack parked in front where he could keep an eye on his unit and we got out and went inside.

The smell of heaven greeted us as we walked in, and it seemed to be popular as most of the booths were taken. It had an organic, modern farmhouse vibe with a lot of shiplap, exposed wood, and industrial pipes. They sold homemade crocks of butter and specialty breads, and they sold coffee by the pound in recycled flour sacks.

"Trendy," Jack said. "You order. I'll get a table. They haven't arrived yet."

Their menu seemed overly complicated so I got two black coffees and resisted the temptation of the bakery goods displayed in the glass-front cabinet. Jack had managed to find an empty corner booth and he sat with his back to the wall so he could see the front door. When he saw me approaching, he got out of the booth so I could slide in.

"There they are," Jack said, nodding to the door. "This is very good coffee, by the way."

"You might not say that if you knew how much it cost," I said. "He put his hand on her back."

"What?" Jack asked, looking at me curiously.

"He touched her," I said. "A guy doesn't touch a girl like that unless they've been intimate."

"Hmm," Jack said.

"It's true," I said. "People always give intimacy

away, even when they're trying not to. They're a couple."

Savannah went to the counter to order while Jaden came our way. "Thanks for meeting with us," he said, sliding into the booth.

"Like I said," Jack told him. "We were already on campus, so it's not a problem."

He wore a beanie cap pulled over his bright red hair, and I noticed he was dressed a little more on the goth side of things from when I'd seen him two days before. He still had the same cocky grin, but his black flannel, jeans, and combat boots looked like he'd salvaged them from his dad's closet in 1996.

Savannah was wearing an almost identical outfit, but her nails were painted black and her nose had a tiny diamond stud in it. She handed Jaden his coffee and then sat next to him.

"Why don't y'all tell us why you wanted to meet," Jack said, starting the conversation.

"Have you found out anything more about what happened to Kevin?" Savannah asked, both hands wrapped around her cup.

"We're finding out more every day," Jack told her. "Were you and Kevin close? I noticed you were the one most upset when we spoke the other day."

"That's just because she's got a heart," Jaden said, grinning. "All the other guys are mostly robots. They're not really good with feelings and emotions."

"Kevin was like a big brother," she said. "He and

Dwight both were like that. More mature, I guess. Kind of like mentors. It was hard to follow in their footsteps. Especially Kevin's. He was something special."

"Did he have any serious enemies? Anyone make threats on the message boards or online?" Jack asked.

"There's always trash talk," Jaden said. "It's just part of the game. But probably his biggest enemy was that guy Chad. What he did to Kevin was pretty brutal."

"Do y'all know Chad?" I asked.

"Nah," Jaden said. "I wouldn't even know what he looked like except he was hanging around outside of the building where the Kings meet a couple of times. Madison would wait for Kevin there, but Chad would show up and start yelling, asking her why she was dating a loser like Kev and all this other stuff. Classic bully move."

"What about the sword?" Jack asked. "Did Chad ever see the sword?"

"I don't know," Savannah said. "Maybe. Dwight would bring it to sessions. He wasn't allowed to carry it in the sheath on his back because the university says it's too 'aggressive.'" She rolled her eyes. "So he had this special black case made and carried it in that. If you passed him on the sidewalk, you wouldn't know what was in the case. He mostly only took it out when we were all together."

"Chad's an electrical engineering major," Jack

said. "Could he have done the things to Dwight's sword that you saw at the tournament?"

They both got quiet. Worry flashed in Savannah's eyes, but Jaden said, "Maybe." And left it at that.

"Anyone you can think of that might have access to Dwight's sword?" Jack asked.

"Anyone, I guess," Savannah said. "We're all familiar with it and have touched it. We'll sometimes help him tinker with it, try out different ways to get the sparks he's looking for. But it's all in fun. Nothing serious or harmful."

"Dwight is the only one of us who lives off campus," Jaden said. "We use his place on weekends to do D&D sessions. He keeps the sword in a glass case on display. But it's out of the case more than in it. He likes to play with it."

"You all seemed pretty impressed when you saw what Dwight's sword did at the tournament," Jack said. "You'd never seen it do anything like that before?"

"No way," Jaden said, unable to help his grin of admiration. "It was wicked. Primo science."

"Is Dwight smart enough for that kind of science?" Jack asked.

Jaden shrugged. "I mean, don't get me wrong. Dwight's a genius. But I've never seen any of his experiments or school projects look anything like that. That kind of science is awe inspiring."

"It sounds like you admire whoever did it," Jack said.

"As a scientist," he said. "Yeah, I guess I do."

"I get the feeling there was a reason other than this you wanted to talk," Jack said. "Am I wrong?"

Jaden looked at Savannah and she nodded at him encouragingly.

"You're not wrong," he said. "I just figured I should tell you that I've got a criminal history. I have a juvie record. I went through a rough spell a few years ago and spent some time in the detention center. But that's all in the past. I got things straightened out and haven't had any trouble since. I just wanted to let you know. On the TV shows they always look hardest at the guy who has a record."

"I appreciate the honesty," Jack said. "You both fought in the tournament the other day. Did either of you see Kevin or Dwight around?"

"Yeah, actually," Jaden said. "Midnight and I were the fight right before Kaal and Uridak."

"I remember you said you won," Jack said. "That must have put a strain on your relationship."

Savannah looked down at her coffee and Jaden's cheeks turned as bright as his hair, and then he cleared his throat and said, "Ahh, the relationship part is kind of new. You really start to reevaluate things when someone you know dies like that."

Savannah peeked up at him out of the corner of her eye and reached out and took his hand, squeezing it gently.

"What did you see after your round of the fight?" Jack asked.

"Midnight and I were heading back to the

dressing area, and I saw Kevin coming out of Dwight's dressing room. He looked upset."

"Did he say anything to you?" I asked.

"Nothing," Jaden said. "I don't even think he saw me. He had tunnel vision. I could tell something was wrong. But he just went back to his dressing room and closed the door. I should have said something to him. I didn't know it was the last time I'd see him alive."

CHAPTER TWELVE

"IT'S GETTING DARK," JACK SAID AFTER WE'D LEFT Jaden and Savannah. "I guess we should stop by the grocery store and pick up food for Doug and Ryan before they eat the furniture."

My phone rang at that moment and I looked at the caller ID. It was from the hospital. Which meant someone was dead.

"Dr. Graves," I said, answering, and then I listened while the information was relayed and said, "I'll be there in twenty." I looked at Jack. "Looks like you're going to have to hit the store by yourself. I've got to go pick up a body at the hospital morgue. Fourteen-year-old girl collapsed at the lunch table at school and teachers called an ambulance, but she was pronounced dead by the time she got to the hospital and before the parents could arrive. They asked for an autopsy to find cause of death, and I need to get it done quickly."

"I guess that's a good excuse for getting out of grocery shopping," Jack said. "I hate it when it's kids. I'll drop you off and pick you up in a couple hours."

"I'll just drive the Suburban home. No need for you to get back out again. Just promise me you won't buy only healthy stuff at the grocery store. You don't want our house to turn into *Lord of the Flies*."

"I can't make any promises," Jack said.

I was back at the funeral home with the body in less than an hour. They'd had her and the paperwork ready for me as soon as I'd backed the Suburban up to the loading dock. But it was the phone call I'd made on my way home that had me biting my lip with nerves. I'd learned over the past year that sometimes you couldn't do it all, and it was okay to ask for help. Sometimes.

"Please come back to work," I begged Lily when she picked up the phone. "But for pay this time instead of being an intern. Wait, let me finish before you say no. You don't even have to come back full time. You can work around your doctoral work and your hours at the body farm. Whatever you need, you've got it. You call the shots. Please..."

There was silence on the other end of the line.

"Did you hang up?" I asked softly.

Lily laughed and said, "No, I was just waiting to

see if you'd passed out from not taking a breath. I thought you got a new intern and didn't need me anymore."

"I definitely need you," I said. "I punched the new intern in the jaw and kneed him in the balls. Our working relationship is strained. Not to mention the fact he belongs in jail."

"Yikes," Lily said. "Let me guess. Blake Steed. I've heard plenty of rumors but nothing ever came of it. He always steered clear of me."

"That is odd," I said. "He didn't waste any time with me. I don't know what he was thinking. He couldn't possibly believe I'd have anything to do with him. He was totally delusional."

"He's got a god complex," Lily said. "He thought he was something in the pathology department at school too. The professors loved him. The rest of us spent a lot of time rolling our eyes. Do you really want me to work for you? For real?"

"For real," I said. "I didn't realize how much of my work has shifted from funeral home work to county coroner work. Last year was a good balance. I finally felt like I was able to do justice to both of the hats I wear, but it was only because I had good help."

She let out a sigh of relief. "I'm so glad you called," she said. "This program is kicking my butt, and I need something to break up the monotony of endless studying. I miss working hands on. When do you want me to start?"

"You don't want to ask how much you're being paid?" I asked.

"Since I was making nothing as an intern, I'm good with anything above zero dollars. When do you want me to start?"

"I don't suppose you could start now," I said tentatively. "I just picked up a body from the morgue at the hospital."

"I can be there in ten minutes," she said. "Cole got called out to a scene, so no telling when he'll be back. Could be an hour. Might be two days from now. And I've already cleaned his house and snooped through his things, so I'm kinda bored now."

"Ahh, the fun life of loving a cop," I said. "See you in ten."

Lily's little red car was parked in front of the funeral home when I pulled into the carport, and she was sitting in the front seat with the heater running to stay warm.

Dusk was just beginning to fall and the streetlights on the corners flickered on as I made my way down Catherine of Aragon and turned into the drive. I pulled under the carport, and Lily met me at the back.

She was dressed in a puffy blue coat with a pretty fur hood and jeans, and she looked like she'd just stepped off the pages of an L.L. Bean catalog. All I could do was pull her into a hug.

"It's good to see you," I said.

"It's good to be back. It's been a while since I had my hands in a body. All this academic research stuff is boring me to tears. What's the deal with the victim?" she asked. "You usually don't start autopsies this late unless it's urgent. Is it a homicide?"

"Not this one," I said. "Fourteen-year-old girl collapsed at school for no reason. No past medical issues and nothing from the external that anyone could see. She just died for no reason."

"I hate it when it's kids," Lily said, opening the back gate of the Suburban.

We slid out the gurney and rolled her up the ramp and into the funeral home, and I locked the door behind us and set the alarm out of habit. We stopped and hung our coats and bags in the mudroom and then rolled the gurney the rest of the way into the kitchen.

I typed the code in the keypad that opened the lab door and we rolled the gurney into the elevator. I rode down with the victim while Lily took the stairs.

The good thing about having Lily back in the lab was that she knew my habits and didn't have to ask a lot of questions. Things were just done when they were supposed to be done and it made the whole process a lot quicker.

"Charlotte Vickery," I said, reading the hospital

paperwork. "Let's find out what happened to you, Charlotte."

We had her opened up on the table in no time, and I was examining and weighing the organs when the alarm went off signaling the initial tox screen had finished being analyzed. I had a few more abilities in my lab than most, and I could get a more in-depth report than basic drugs or alcohol.

"Not even a little blip," Lily said, looking at the computer screen. "Nothing remotely odd in her system."

"Her heart looks good too," I said. "No cardiac arrest. No anomalies or tumors in any of the other organs. Which leaves us with the brain."

It was there we found cause of death. A pinprick aneurism that had ruptured, killing her almost instantly. There would have been no reason for anyone to have even known it was there.

"Well," Lily said. "At least the parents will know why. Sometimes knowing brings a little bit of comfort."

For some people it did. But their daughter would always be dead, and there was a helplessness in knowing there was nothing anyone could have done about it. If she'd been standing in the hospital, she still probably would have died. It was these events that always reminded me of the fragileness of the human body, and how intricately complicated our design.

I signed off on the autopsy report and scanned it and sent it back to the hospital, and then we cleaned up and rolled her into the cooler next to Kevin Schwartzman. Jack called just as I closed the cooler door.

"Perfect timing," I said. "Just finished up here."

"That was fast," Jack said. "I was going to tell you I was on the way to get you."

"I told you I could take the Suburban home," I said. "I don't want you to have to get out again."

"Two things," Jack said. "I don't want you leaving by yourself after dark with Blake out there. The deputies I sent out to bring him in couldn't pin him down today. He never went back home. And second, Doug hasn't stopped talking since I got back. I don't mind having to get out again. Really, it's no trouble."

I snickered and followed Lily up the stairs and into the kitchen. "Lily is here," I said. "And we're just about to walk it. I'm ready to be home. I don't want to wait twenty minutes for you to get here."

"Why is Lily there?" Jack asked.

"She was driving by and felt the need to do an autopsy."

"As one does," Jack said, making me laugh.

"I called her and begged her to come to work full time," I said. "Which reminds me, I need you to call the accountant and have him work up something magical as far as paying her goes."

"You have the number for the accountant too," Jack said.

"Yes, but I always feel like a fraud when I call

him. I'm still not used to having a business that runs in the black. I'm afraid I'll screw it up."

"You're so weird," Jack said. "But I love you anyway. Hurry home."

We disconnected and I told Lily, "Just message me your schedule and we'll work something out. I don't want you to get overwhelmed. It's not like we have a murder every day."

"No, but with the influx of people trying to escape DC to the quiet life, crime is definitely on the rise. I'll make you a deal—I'll give you a few hours a week to help out around the funeral home, but you call me immediately whenever a homicide comes in. If I can stop what I'm doing, I'll be here."

"Deal," I said. "I'll take whatever pieces of you are left."

"I guess that makes me vulture meat," she said teasingly. "Fortunately, there's enough of me to go around." She looked out the window of the back door. "I really hate the winter." She took her jacket from the hook and put it on and then grabbed her purse. "You coming?"

"Go ahead and get going," I said. "I'm going to turn the lights off and lock up, but I'm right behind you. Be careful driving. The roads might be slick in places."

"I'm just heading back to Cole's house. He's right around the corner. Besides, he owes me a romantic dinner and a lot of sex."

"I'd shower first and get the autopsy smell off you."

"That's why you're my mentor," she said, giving me a cheeky grin and a wave goodbye.

I turned off the lights and grabbed my own coat and bag, knocking something to the floor in the process. Lily's wallet must have fallen out of her purse and onto the bench, but it had gotten stuck in my coat. I put the wallet in my bag and set the alarm, and then I dug out my cell phone so I could text Lily before she got too far to let her know she'd forgotten it.

My head was buried in my phone when I shut the door behind me and rattled the handle to make sure it was locked. I was down the ramp and almost on top of him before I realized Blake Steed was leaning against the hood of the Suburban.

The sight of him surprised me so much that I dropped my keys, and the sound of them hitting the pavement was jarring. I didn't dare bend down to pick them up, but I kept my eyes on his.

"Seems like you're a hard man to track down," I said, deciding to go in with a lot of bravado and bully my way out of the situation if I could. "The police have been looking for you."

"I know," he said. "It's a shame you felt you had to go that route. Women like you make me sick. I thought you'd be different. You're mature. A professional. And you seem to know what you want. But in the end you're all the same. Women just like to play the victim and ruin people's lives."

"Is that right, Travis?" I asked, using his real name. "Tell that to the woman you killed."

The shock was evident on his face, and I was terrified by the look of rage that came across it. It was the look of someone who lacked all sanity or sense of reason. While he grappled with the realization that I knew who he was, I took the opportunity to slide my way toward the back end of the Suburban so someone might see us if they passed by on the street, but Bloody Mary wasn't known for having a bustling night life.

"I don't know a Travis," he said, following me with slow deliberate steps. The rage disappeared from his face as if had never been there. "You must be mistaking me for someone else. I just came to talk and try to get you to see reason. We can move slower in our relationship if that's what you want. Remember you're the one who came on to me." He held up his hands in a surrender pose. "I'm just trying to read all the signals."

"You must have done terrible at your driving test," I said.

He kept talking as if he hadn't heard me. "I'll be here every day and we can get to know each other better as we work. I'm a lot better than Lily. To be honest, I really felt they could have sent you a much better intern last year. But there's nothing to worry about. I'm here now."

Lily's car was no longer parked on the street, and there was no traffic. It was just me and him. After I'd almost died by Jeremy Mooney's hands a couple of years ago, I never went anywhere without my Beretta. I always kept it close at hand. But after

Jack and I had married I'd started to go without it more and more, until it was no longer a habit. Until it was no longer a part of me. I guess I stopped carrying it because I always felt so safe with Jack. But now it was sitting inside the console of the Suburban, doing me a fat lot of good in my current situation.

"Why don't we go in and have a cup of coffee?" he asked. "I know how much you love it. It'll help settle your nerves."

"That's not going to happen," I said, taking another step back. I was standing out from under the carport now in the glow of the streetlight.

"You can't outrun me you know," he said conversationally. "I'm in excellent shape. Obvious-ly." He spread his arms, emphasizing the muscles in his shoulders and arms. And it was then I realized he wasn't wearing a jacket. I guess the crazy was keeping him warm.

I still had my phone in my hand, but I didn't dare take my eyes off him to call Jack, so instead I pressed the side button on my phone a few times to activate the emergency button. I felt the phone buzz in my hand as it gave a countdown before it called 911 on my behalf. Thank God for modern technology.

"Why'd you pick such a stupid name?" I asked. "You had the chance to start over and pick a whole new life. And that's the name you picked?"

His mouth pressed into a thin line of anger, and I could see his shoulders moving as he tried to control his breathing. "Blake was my father's name," he said. "Don't ever say anything bad about my father. I'm losing patience with you. I feel like I've been very understanding, but I don't think you're a very nice person at all."

"You don't think *I'm* a nice person?" I asked. "You spend all your time terrorizing women. Cops are on the way. Better walk away while you can."

"Don't lie," he said, taking a couple of steps toward me. "I hate liars. You're not like the other girls. I tried to be gentle with them so it was beautiful. But I think you deserve the pain."

"That's what you get for picking a woman to tangle with instead of innocent girls," I said, my anger starting to rise above my fear. "You deserve the darkest cell they can throw you in. Living there for eternity with that stupid name is almost punishment enough for you."

He growled and lunged at me, and I spun on my heel and started to run. I didn't know how far away the police would be or if they'd heard the conversation, but if I could just make it a couple of blocks toward the Towne Square where the traffic was heavier I'd be okay.

I felt the twist in my knee even as I had the thought, and I hit the ground hard, scraping my hands on the concrete. And then I heard the squeal of tires and the glare of headlights blasted right in my face as a little red car drove across my lawn and hit Blake Steed right in the shins hard enough to bounce off the windshield.

He lay on the ground unmoving, and Lily swung open her car door and got out, a wild-eyed look on her face.

"I forgot my wallet," she said.

And even though the pain in my knee was excruciating, I started to laugh and couldn't seem to stop.

CHAPTER THIRTEEN

"Put this on your knee," Lily said, getting a bag of peas from the freezer.

Between her and Martinez, they'd managed to help me hobble back into the kitchen and onto a barstool. I situated one of the other barstools so I could prop my leg up and hissed out a sigh when the cold bag of peas rested on my knee.

"I called the sheriff for you," Martinez said, shaking his head as he stared at my knee. "He's on his way. That knee looks nasty. You might have the EMTs look at it."

"I just twisted it," I said. "The EMTs are better off spending their time on Blake."

"You'll be lucky if it doesn't swell up like a grapefruit," Lily said. I noticed her hands were shaking slightly, and she was trying to stay busy so she didn't freak out. "Ohmigod, I just ran over that man with my car. I mean, he deserved it, but I'm never going to get that sound out of my head. Did you see his shoes fly off when he flipped up in the air?"

Martinez snorted. "It's not funny, but if anyone deserved it this guy did. You did the world a service."

"Until some judge puts him back on the street again," I said, pulling at the fabric that had shredded around my knee. The blood was starting to dry and I didn't want it to stick.

"That's the justice system for you," Martinez said. "We can only arrest them. Somebody else gets to be the judge and jury."

"I'll be right back," Lily said. She typed in the code for the lab and disappeared for a few minutes. When she came back her arms were full of bandages and antiseptic.

"Do you want to give your statement now or wait until the sheriff arrives?" Martinez asked.

"Might as well wait so I don't have to give it twice," I said. "How bad are Blake's injuries?"

"Not bad enough as far as I'm concerned," Martinez said. "He's still breathing. Other than that, he's got a broken leg, lots of scrapes and bruises, and his brain got scrambled some. Next time aim for his penis."

"I'll make sure to buy a taller car for next time," Lily said dryly. "Let me clean your hands first." She laid out all the supplies on the island and I held out my hands palms up so she could clean the dirt and grime out of the wounds.

The door opened and I looked over expectantly, hoping it was Jack, but it was Detective Cole. He must have come straight from whatever scene he'd been working. He was in regular attire of jeans and cowboy boots, and he wore a sport coat to cover his holster. His expression was strained as he looked Lily over from head to toe to make sure she was all right.

"I'm fine," she said. "Just a little shaken up. I've never run over anyone with a car before. I'm sure I'll be fine once the adrenaline passes."

"I can't imagine running someone over is something that happens that often around here," Martinez said.

"Blanche Bourgeois," Cole said. "Back in 1987. I was just a kid, but I remember it well. She had a habit of running over her husbands. Didn't get arrested until after the third one died. You didn't grow up in Bloody Mary, but I can assure you if there's a weird way to murder someone, the citizens here have done it."

"Good to know," Martinez said.

Cole came over and gave Lily a gentle kiss on the forehead and then leaned his head against hers. It was a strangely intimate gesture for Cole, and I wondered if things were more serious between them than any of us realized.

"I'm glad you're okay," Cole said. And then he looked at me. "You too, Doc."

"Gee, thanks, Cole," I said.

"Anytime, sugar," he said, winking.

"Flirt with your own woman," Jack said, closing the kitchen door. I hadn't even heard him come in.

Jack stood in the threshold of the mudroom and stared at me. The scar on his eyebrow was white and his mouth was pressed in a tight line. He saw the peas on my knee and the blood and scraped skin on my hands, and he raised his eyebrow in question.

"I'm okay," I told him. "Just a little scraped up."

"That knee looks more than scraped up," he said, coming into the room. "You need to see a doctor."

I rolled my eyes. "I am a doctor. I just twisted it. It's nothing a little ice won't cure, but I'm going to be stiff and sore for a few days. That's it. I promise. The guy lying on the grass out there is the one who needs a doctor."

"He'll see one right before he goes to jail," Jack said.

"I talked to the dean and president at the university today," Martinez said. "They weren't happy to see a warrant for Blake Steed's file, but you could tell they weren't too surprised by it either. They let campus police handle all of the complaints against Steed."

"And let me guess," Jack said. "They sat on the information."

"Bingo," Martinez said.

"Why would campus police do that?" Lily asked.

"Because the fewer crime campus police reports," Jack said, "the better it looks for the university and enrollment. And enrollment means money. Occasionally we get a student who comes and files a report with us instead of campus police, and then we find out there's been past issues that have never been dealt with or that the university decided to handle academically. It's why the sheriff's office hasn't had the best relationship with campus police in the past."

"Speaking of," Martinez said, "I paid a visit to the new chief. He's no pushover. I explained the issue and told him we'd gotten a warrant for the kid's student file and he told us the name wasn't familiar to him since he'd only been in charge since August, but he ran a search for us."

"And how many women has he victimized?" I asked.

"Wachowski and I talked to twelve today," Martinez said. "Chief Slack was furious. I'd be shaking in my boots if I were Jim Coleman and anyone else who tried to cover this up."

"Good for Slack," Jack said, approvingly. "What about the twelve women?"

"They ran the gauntlet of scared, pissed, and way beyond pissed, but they are more than willing to give formal statements and testify if need be. I think by the time this is finished there's going to be some turnover at the university. Why anyone would let a monster like Blake Steed have free rein on campus blows my mind."

"Why anyone would name themselves Blake Steed blows mine," Lily said.

By the time Lily and I gave our official statements, Blake and most of the cops that had arrived on scene were gone. I held out my hand to Jack so he could help me up, but he didn't take it. Instead he scooped me up in his arms and carried me toward the door.

"My hero," I said, laying my head on his chest. "I'm sorry I wasn't paying closer attention. I got sloppy. My gun was in the car."

"Mmhmm," he said. "You've had a lot of close calls over the last year, and the work we do is dangerous enough that you should always carry. I'm not equipped to dealing with you not being in my life. Stop taking chances. If you can't do it for you then do it for me."

The comment felt like lead weight in my gut. He was right. Despite the chaos we'd been through the last couple of years, I'd attributed most of it to my parents and the danger that they'd brought down on my life. I hadn't really thought about the danger that my own career path brought. I was a sworn officer of the law. I still considered my real job to be that of a mortician and running the funeral home, and coroner was something I treated as an extra. Something that allowed Jack and me to spend more time together. But the truth was, as the county had grown and crime had increased, I spent more time with my coroner hat on. And my name was in the paper or on the news at least once a week.

"I can do it for you," I told him softly. "I'm sorry."

Cole opened the door for Jack, and Lily set the alarm and locked everything up.

"How's your case going?" Jack asked Cole.

"Like most domestics," Cole said. "Husband beat the hell out of her, and she answers the door all bloody and bruised and says nothing is wrong. And that there was no need for the neighbors to call the cops. I took Plank with me because he's all bright and shiny in his uniform and I figured he'd be seen as weak." Cole smiled then and held out his hand to Lily as we made our way down the ramp and to our respective vehicles.

"Man, you should have seen it," Cole said. "Husband got all righteous about how we have no business interfering with a marriage and all this other garbage, and I let him know we're going to arrest him because it's obvious he's beat the hell out of her, and her blood is on his shirt and his knuckles are bloody. Whether she presses charges is up to her, but for now he has to come with us.

"Plank looks at the wife and tells her to go get some clothes on and that she's going to the hospital to be checked out. She's got a broken nose that's so obvious anyone could see, but you can tell she's afraid to take a step in any direction. And the husband tells her she's fine and to go take a shower, and he kind of pushes her out of the way. But she's so weak a strong wind could've knocked her over, so she crashes into the wall and goes down to the ground. Then Plank goes to take down the guy, but gives the guy a chance to evade first."

Jack grinned and said, "That's my boy."

"And the husband plows his fist right into Plank's jaw, and Plank just stands there like he didn't even feel it. So I move in to assist, and then Plank does this crazy takedown and manages to knock the wind out of him, give him a shot to the kidney and break his finger all at the same time. He's got the guy flat on his face and in cuffs before you can say *howdoyado*."

"Sorry I missed it," Jack said.

"He's got it on body cam," Cole said. "I'm sure he'll be playing multiple showings at the station tomorrow. The wife won't press charges, and now she's mad at us because her husband's in jail. We've got him on evading and assaulting an officer."

Jack sighed and shook his head. "He'll be out after a few months and back to tormenting her unless we can get her with a women's shelter or a social worker. I'll put in a call tomorrow and see if she'll accept help. That's all we can do."

Cole's police unit was parked in front of the funeral home and Jack was parked behind him.

Lily sighed. "My poor car," she said. "Running over people is not good for a grad student's budget."

"Well, you probably saved my life," I said. "And at least you have a paying job now. I wouldn't worry too much about your car. They towed it over to the mechanic and it'll be good as new."

"Need any help with the wizard murder?" Cole asked.

"I'll let you know," Jack said. "We're past the twenty-four-hour mark and our suspect list has grown larger rather than smaller."

"Sounds about right," Cole said, and he and Lily said their goodnights.

I must've fallen asleep on the drive home because Jack was leaning in to pick me up and he startled me awake.

"Easy," he said. "It's just me."

"You don't have to carry me," I said. "I can walk."

"Not well, and it's cold. Let's get inside and get you to bed."

"I think I'm too tired to be trifled with tonight," I said.

Jack snorted out a laugh. "Trifled with?"

"You know what I mean," I said. "I'm going to have to postpone nighttime activities until I have a full range of motion."

"Just to be clear," Jack said. "You don't need a full range of motion. I can do the work for both of us. But trifling with you was not on my mind at the moment. I was thinking you needed to go to bed and sleep."

"I'm fine," I said. "I'm awake. I just need a muscle relaxer and something to reduce the inflammation and I'll be good to go. We've still got work to do tonight, and I'm not going to miss out while you and Doug have all the fun."

Jack sighed and said, "I figured that's what you would say." And he carried me into the house.

"Are we going to take care of Lily's car?" I asked.

"I'll buy her a whole new one," he said. "She's a hero."

"Whoa," Doug said, coming out of the kitchen when he heard the door open. "Look what the cat dragged in. What happened to you?"

"Got chased down by a serial rapist," I said. "And then Lily ran over him with her car."

"Wicked," Doug said. "Very sexy. I like dangerous women."

"She'd eat you alive," I said.

"That's the point," Doug said, waggling his eyebrows. "You're out of peanut butter by the way."

"I just bought that jar today," Jack said, taking me into the office and sitting me in the oversized corner chair.

"Yeah, have you noticed how they're putting less and less food into containers but charging the same price?" Doug asked. "Drives me crazy. Mom always buys two of everything."

"Good to know," Jack said.

"What happened with the sword?" I asked. "Did you and Ryan find out anything?"

"First of all," Doug said. "She's awesome. Like one of those cranky old women who sits on her porch and yells at the kids walking by. But she's super smart too. Not as smart as me, but pretty smart. She knows about video games and how to take apart all kinds of kitchen appliances."

"If you took apart any of my kitchen appliances to make robots it's not going to be good for you," Jack said. "I'm pretty sure I made that clear the last time you came and tried to do that."

"Relax," Doug said. "No one tampered with your appliances. But your oven heats up twice as fast now. We got tired of waiting for the pizza rolls to be done."

"Maybe you should just tell us about the sword," I said.

"Like, totally righteous," Doug said, flopping backward onto the couch and propping his feet up. "I almost hated to take it apart until I realized what it was."

"And what was that?" Jack asked.

"It's a hologram," he said.

"A hologram didn't kill Kevin Schwartzman," I said. "Electricity did."

"Yeah, but that part was nothing special," he said, shrugging. "Ryan and I watched some tape of the other tournaments this year, and Uridak's sword did shoot off sparks, but it wasn't a constant current like the one that runs when you flip the switch now. Once we took the sword apart, we found remnants of what he'd previously used. Just a simple science fair project, two exposed wires that touched to make sparks. He'd added a sound box to get the crazy movie sound effects. You can even see the tips of the wires in one of the videos."

"So what changed, and what's the hologram have to do with anything?" I asked.

"Once we took apart the sword, it was easy to see someone had wired up what's basically a cattle prod. Only a cattle prod delivers about 4,500 to 5000 volts when it makes contact. For comparison, a police taser delivers about 50,000 volts but it drops to 1,200 once contact is made with the skin.

"But anyone one who paid attention in middle school science knows that it's not volts that will kill you. It's the current. We tested the volts and it rang in at just under 50,000 volts. Now in a contest like this, it's still illegal because just the touch is enough to incapacitate the opponent so extra blows can be gotten in. But it shouldn't be fatal unless there's a heart condition or something like that. Similar to a taser.

"But if you're working with that much voltage, you're either a complete idiot or you know exactly what you're doing. Because the current that the voltage delivers has to have a place to go. And if the body is grounded, and Kaal Dracarian, the current would go straight through his body and out his shoes. I'm assuming that's what happened?"

I nodded and Jack hit a button on the computer, and he put the photo of Kevin's shoes I'd taken at the autopsy up on the whiteboard.

Doug nodded as if he'd have expected nothing less.

"The problem was that Kaal Dracarian uses metal armor," he said. "It's legendary. You can look up the exact specs and see photographs online, so it's not like it's a big surprise. And again, anyone who knows anything about science, and I expect all of your suspects do, would know that with all that metal containing the current, that it would probably have a field day dancing around in his system before finding the outlet to escape."

"There was no damage done to his organs," I told Doug. "The last time I worked a lightning strike victim all the internal organs looked like someone had put them in the microwave too long and they exploded."

"Gross," Doug said, but with the same enthusiasm he used when saying something was awesome.

"That's an understatement," I said.

"That's the cool thing about electricity," Doug said. "Lightning never strikes the same way twice. And it's the same with being electrocuted. There are so many elements involved. You're not only dealing with currents and voltage, but also with man-made materials like his clothing and even what the floor was made of. It all affects what the current will do. The current bounced around and cooked him in that metal armor, but by the time it found an outlet there was no chance of reviving him."

"I still don't understand what the hologram has to do with anything," Jack said.

"Don't you see?" Doug asked.

"Obviously not," Jack said, raising his brows threateningly at Doug.

Doug just grinned, enjoying the attention. "It's like a calling card. Holograms take a very specific know-how of physics and engineering. Most colleges don't even have hologram programs because the equipment is so expensive, and it's not a huge field of study so professors are hard to find. It's not something you just learn how to do in your spare time. It takes math and physics and formulas and equipment. You find who can produce a hologram like that and you'll find your killer."

"Dwight Parr won that Archimedes Fellowship at Oxford," I said.

"Yeah, in electrical engineering," Doug said. "I doubt you'll find anything linking him to this kind of science. Check his research papers, talk to his professors. It'll be very clear what his area of study is. This is one of those things where you'll know it when you see it."

CHAPTER FOURTEEN

DOUG LEFT TO GO PLAY VIDEO GAMES FOR THE REST of the night, and Jack updated the information we had for the murder board.

"Madison Marbury definitely has a reason to kill Kevin," I said as he added to her file. "And she's a math major."

"But she must not be that great of one since she went to Kevin for tutoring. But her motive is the strongest. It's possible she could've had help though. Just like she helped Chad with his prank."

Jack attached the first video of her and Kevin so the folder popped up under her picture, and then he did a search for Kevin's revenge video. It didn't take long to find. It was everywhere, and a second folder popped up under her picture.

"Angry women can be very resourceful," I said.

"Agreed," Jack said. "Jim Coleman sent over the student files we requested. Let's check hers out."

Another screen came up on the wall and Madison's digital file came into view. Her student ID picture was there along with her transcript, medical, and any academic correspondence.

"You're right," I said. "Her grades are average at best, even lower in her weaker subjects. I'm surprised she's trying to go on to grad school. Look at her medical file."

Jack hit the medical tab and the screen changed. A lot more information appeared than what was on her transcript. "Looks like she's a frequent visitor. What's benzodiazepine?"

"It's for anxiety or panic attacks," I said, shifting in the chair so I could see better. "And look at the date."

"Not long after the video of her and Kevin went viral," Jack said.

"She's got several prescriptions for birth control pills over the past couple of years," I said. "And it looks like she's struggled with stress or anxiety in the past. She's got a couple of different concoctions in there for nerves. Antibiotics freshman year because of pneumonia, and she got her flu shot every year." I scanned the lines, but didn't see anything too out of the ordinary. "What's her most recent visit?"

"She's been four times since December," Jack said. He clicked on the paperwork from her first visit in December.

"That's just a few weeks ago," I said. "Severe vomiting, weight loss, stress. The date coincides with when Kevin released his revenge video. She was given Phenergan for the nausea and told to rest through the holidays. It looks like she came back as soon as the clinic opened again after the New Year."

"Uh-oh," Jack said, bringing the next document up on screen. "I guess her birth control pills didn't work."

"No, look," I said. "Look at the date of her last prescription. She stopped taking them all together."

"Why would she get pregnant on purpose?" Jack asked.

"She said she thought Kevin was going to propose to her," I said. "Maybe she wanted to ensure it. Or maybe she was tired of school. She wasn't great at it, but a girl like Madison would know that Kevin was brilliant and he would be able to provide for her and a child. What are the other visits?"

"Looks like general checkups," Jack said. "Still having trouble with the nausea, and still losing weight. This only adds to her motive for killing him, or finding someone to do it for her. Talk about a woman scorned."

"We need to find out if she had access to the weapon in any way. When we spoke with her all she said was that the Kings were weirdos and they stuck together. But according to everyone else, Kevin and Dwight were close. She'd have at least met him or hung out with him from time to time."

"We need to find out who had most recent

access to Dwight's sword," I said. "Everyone knew it was his. They're all familiar with it."

"We can talk to him in the morning before we interview Chad Wheeler," Jack said. "I want to ask him about the holograms or if he knows anyone whose area of study is holograms."

"You don't think it was Dwight?" I asked. "He's an electrical engineering major."

"I'm not ruling out the possibility, but no, I don't think it was Dwight. I think Dwight was just a means to an end and a convenient scapegoat. But talking to him tomorrow will give me a better idea. We didn't get a lot out of him during our first conversation. He's got nothing on his record—no skirmishes with the law or underage drinking, not even a parking ticket. He lives in one of those mixed-use buildings about a block from campus over a Korean barbecue restaurant. The team did a search through his apartment, but there was no evidence that he'd been tinkering with the sword. He had bits and pieces of different costumes, a bunch of drawings of different weapons, and little projects he was tinkering with, but nothing concrete. The techs picked up several sets of prints all over the apartment, including the glass case where he kept the sword, so it confirms what Jaden and Savannah told us about hanging out there for D&D sessions."

"Or maybe they told us that we'd find their prints for another reason," I said. "Were there any prints on the exterior of the sword?"

"Nothing," Jack said. "Not even Dwight's. He was wearing gloves. But it's time to start breaking down the Kings. We'll interview them individually starting tomorrow. I want to know who had access to the sword, and who will benefit most from Kevin's death. His parents had a small insurance policy on him, but other than that, no one gains financially through life insurance or an estate. The only financial gain would be through the scholarship. And that goes to Dwight."

"Who can't use it when he goes to Oxford next year," I said.

"Right."

"Any hits on the background checks for the Kings?" I asked.

"A few blips here and there," Jack said, and then he hit a few keys on the keyboard and things started popping up on the murder board. "Miley George is an applied mathematics and engineering double major. She's a junior, and she has an underage drinking charge from early in her freshman year. She had to do community service, but no time served.

"Nikhil Noriega must have been at the same party because he got the same punishment, only his was more severe because he had a few joints in his pocket. He's also a junior and an engineering major, so they'll have some of the same classes together I'm assuming. Between applied mathematics and engineering maybe one of them has a clue how to make a hologram."

"It'd be interesting to see them working on anything after watching them interact with each other yesterday," I said. "They're all competitive, but I get the feeling the only reason they're a group is because that's how it's structured by the university. They all seem like the type of people who'd rather work on their own than with a partner."

"But they said they sometimes use each other as a sounding board for ideas and strategy. Maybe that extends to school projects or experiments outside of the Kings."

"It's definitely worth looking into," I said. "But remember that Miley is one of the top ten players and Nikhil isn't. I wouldn't think she'd want to see him advance above her."

"I wonder if there's a team prize," Jack said. "In some sports you have the individual events, but you also have a team score. I wonder if the university gets anything out of this."

"Sounds like a question for your buddy Jim," I said.

Jack pressed his lips together in annoyance. "He's not my buddy," he said. "Moving on, Savannah Rowe is clean. Looks like she's lived a pretty sheltered life. Only child. Parents are well off financially. Doesn't look like she needs the money for tuition. She's the youngest of the group as a sophomore. There's nothing in her file that she didn't tell us over coffee. Physics major. Good student."

"And infatuated with Jaden," I said. "The way

she was looking at him today was almost painful to watch."

Jack's lip twitched. "Sex is a powerful bonding agent. Especially for a woman. None of these guys strike me as overly astute when it comes to the opposite sex. But Savannah seems like the most human of the bunch. They'll figure out the boy/girl dance in the next decade or so."

The wall of whiteboard was starting to fill up. We had too many suspects, and we were going to have to figure out who to focus on so we didn't waste time and resources. And we were going to have to do it soon. By morning we'd be past the thirty-six-hour mark and no closer to finding out who murdered Kevin Schwartzman.

"It's probably a good thing Jaden Matthews gave us a heads-up about his misspent youth," Jack said. "His juvie record is sealed. I'm going to go through the proper channels and file for a subpoena to open it up, but since it's the weekend, it'll be Monday before I can have it in hand. Just to make sure that there's nothing to tie him to this crime. I'll have Carver go ahead and expedite the process while we're waiting on the court."

"It'll give him something to do," I said.

"Yeah, for about five minutes," Jack replied. "Good thing he's got his High Council to fall back on to keep him busy."

I snickered and said, "Isn't Jaden Matthews a grad student? He and Savannah might be only a year or two off in age difference, but in education he's light-years ahead. He might have the advanced knowledge to show an interest in holograms. What does his student file say?"

Jack pulled up the file on Jaden Matthews. "He enrolled as a freshman at KGU at sixteen and finished his undergrad at nineteen. He's still shy of his twenty-first birthday. Mother is an astrophysicist and father is a theoretical physicist. And he's ranked number four on the national LARP rankings."

"It doesn't sound like he'd need the finances that moving to the number one spot would provide," I said.

"Looks like his father was let go from a research facility several years back and now he and the mother both teach college. And Jaden is one of three kids in college. It looks like they could definitely use the financial help."

"What about the last guy?" I asked. "David Englander. As normal as he is, he's the one who doesn't fit in with that group."

"Yeah," Jack said. "It's an odd matchup. He's in the National Guard reserves so he has to report back once a month for training. I'll get a subpoena for his service record just to make sure everything looks good there, but the rest of his record is clean."

Jack rubbed at the back of his neck, and I knew he was tired. Things hadn't lightened up after the election—they'd only grown more intense. Jack loved police work, but it was the administrative and political side of things he could've done without—

the renovation of the jail and sheriff's office, the hiring of new deputies to help with the growing population, the public appearances...the job rarely ended when he walked through the door at the end of the day. Someone always needed something.

"Englander grew up in the system," he continued. "Different foster parents since the age of nine. Life before nine was spent with broken bones and hospital visits—classic signs of childhood abuse and neglect before he was removed from the home permanently.

"He graduated high school and immediately enlisted in the military. He lists his apartment as his permanent address. Doesn't look like he maintains a relationship with any of the foster parents. And he didn't start college until he was twenty-one, so he's older than the others, but they definitely consider him part of the group. Anyone elite enough to make it into the Kings is automatically welcome. You could tell they were bonded together, despite their competitive spirits.

"And on David's side, he seems very comfortable there, despite his age, background, and military history. But it's not uncommon with children of abuse or those who are in the system to want to prolong childhood or immature acts a little longer. They don't mature as fast as their peers do in a stable environment, and they can maintain that level of immaturity well into adulthood, so that very well could explain his need to interact with the gaming crowd or students younger than he is."

Jack's psychology degree came in handy in law enforcement and understanding the human mind —and the criminal mind. It was easy to forget that he was seeing and hearing things totally different than I was while we were listening to the same conversation.

"I'll send Carver a text with what we need until I can get subpoenas," Jack said. "But otherwise, there's not much more we can do until morning. Martinez is bringing in Chad Wheeler, so we can talk with him once we're done with Dwight."

"Do you think there's a possibility that all this was just an accident?" I asked. "That maybe Dwight just wanted to stun his opponent so he could incapacitate him long enough to get the hit points? The scholarship is not the only prize. It's just the prize of whoever keeps the top ranking. The winner of this tournament would've gotten ten thousand dollars plus all these cool gadgets and nerd toys. People have killed over a lot less than that."

"That's true," Jack said, scooping me up in his arms and then turning off the light as we left the office. "But adding the hologram was cocky. Like Doug said, it's a calling card. And I bet at least one of these kids recognizes who it belongs to. And that person will be able to tell us who tampered with that sword. We just have to break them down one by one until someone confesses."

"Speaking of confessions," I said as he started up the stairs.

"Yes?" he asked, stopping halfway up and arching a brow at me in question.

"I might have been a bit hasty in my earlier statement."

Jack's mouth quirked into a smile. "Which statement was that?"

"It seems the muscle relaxer and anti-inflammatory are doing their jobs, and I'd like to be trifled with after all."

I wrapped my arms around his neck and kissed him, nipping at his bottom lip so he hissed out a breath of excitement.

"I promise to be very gentle," he said, kissing me back with a passion that melted my body against his.

"Maybe not too gentle."

CHAPTER FIFTEEN

THE SECOND DAY OF AN INJURY WAS ALWAYS THE worst. As a doctor, I've told that to patients before, but for some reason, I'd totally forgotten it applied to me until I tried to put my feet on the floor the next morning.

"Oh, God," I said, the stiffness in my joints causing me to breathe through the pain. Of course, Jack might have had something to do with the stiffness too. We'd both forgotten the definition of "gentle" sometime during the night.

Jack had put my coffee in its usual place on the nightstand by my side of the bed, but there were also two pills sitting next to the cup. If he'd been in the room, I would've kissed him.

I swallowed the pills and gingerly got to my feet, testing the weight on my knee to see if it would hold me up. I was grateful I'd iced it immediately because it would've been much worse than it was, but I could use it as long as I moved slow and careful, and maybe after a hot shower it would loosen up even more.

I padded to the shower naked, clutching my coffee cup like it was the elixir of life, and using my other hand to steady myself on the furniture. I stopped when I got to the full-length mirror, gasping at the swollen and bruised knee, but also the yellow and purple bruises that had formed all the way up to my hip. I wasn't even sure how the other injuries had happened. My hands were sore, but Lily had bandaged them, and I could feel the warmth from the cup through the gauze.

I turned on the shower and set my coffee on the tiled shelf, and then I carefully unwrapped the bandages and tossed them in the trash. I stared at the deep clawfoot tub for a moment, debating on soaking my whole body in hot water, but I was afraid I'd never be able to get out again. So I stepped into the shower and under the spray.

My coffee kicked in about mid-way through the shower, and I felt almost human by the time I turned the water off and stepped onto the floor mat. My knee was still swollen and painful, but it was usable, and that's all I needed.

The sun was just barely starting to peek over the treetops as I picked out something to wear for the day, but the snow had disappeared from the branches, and the sound of the Potomac's rushing waters was louder than normal from the snow melt off. It was a soothing sound, but Jack had designed every aspect of the house to fit into the landscape—trees, cliffs, and water.

I'd been standing in the closet several minutes when I finally got aggravated with myself and just picked what I thought would be the most comfortable for my knee and bruised body. I found a black stretchy all-purpose skirt that came to mid-calf, and then I spent the next twenty minutes trying to figure out what to wear with it. I was pretty low maintenance in the clothes department since dark pants or a dark suit was generally my work uniform in the funeral business, but the skirt seemed to call for something more fashionable, so I paired it was a pair of buckskin suede boots that stopped below the knee so I could still get them zipped and the matching suede motorcycle-style jacket.

I found a thin-striped black and tan shirt and a wide belt that draped around my hips to complete the outfit. By the time I finished dressing, I was feeling fancy so I figured I might as well spend a little more time on my hair and makeup.

I was on my way down the stairs when I met Jack on the landing.

"Whoa," he said, eyeing me from head to toe and then lingering on my breasts. "I was just coming to see if you needed me to help you down. But I'm thinking now maybe we should go back upstairs. I have something I want to show you."

I snorted out a laugh. "I can only imagine what that could be. But I'll have to take a raincheck. This took way too long to achieve, and I think I've had all the trifling my body will allow."

"Just so I'm covering my bases," he said. "Have I forgotten a special occasion?" He put his arm around my waist and took my weight so I could get downstairs.

"No, one thing just kind of led to another," I explained. "I was looking for something comfortable that wouldn't compress my knee. Thus, the skirt. Things kind of snowballed from there."

"The female mind never ceases to amaze me," Jack said. "I made breakfast tacos."

"I love you," I said with a happy sigh.

"Hopefully for reasons besides tacos," he said.

"Don't forget the trifling." I grinned and then swatted him on the butt when we made it to the bottom of the stairs. "Seriously, sometimes I have to pinch myself. Whatever I did in this life to deserve you I have no idea. But I'm hoping God doesn't realize the mistake anytime soon. You really are the best."

He grinned and leaned down to kiss me—a slow, easy kiss that felt like home and comfort and peace all wrapped into one. Peace wasn't something I'd grown up with or lived with most of my adult life, but now that I knew what it was it was an unmistakable feeling. And I didn't ever want to be without it again.

"I figured Doug would've beaten me to the food," I said, taking a seat gingerly on a bar stool.

"I'm sure he'll be asleep a while longer," Jack

said. "He was up half the night playing video games."

I had a breakfast taco halfway to my mouth when Jack asked, "What do you think about Doug living with us for a while?"

I chewed and tried to focus on the question. Jack was an excellent cook, and food was an experience when he created things in the kitchen.

"He's growing on you, huh?" I asked, taking another bite. "This is really good, by the way."

"He's growing like mold," Jack said teasingly. "And he's driving me crazy." He put coffee in to-go mugs and snapped the lids. "But it's not a bad kind of crazy. It's kind of nice having him here. He's still a kid, but he has an adult mind in certain areas. It's got to be a weird transition. And other than Ben, he doesn't have any male influence in his life. His mom is doing all she can, but most of her time is spent working. And now Ben..."

"I know," I said sympathetically. None of us knew the long-term effects that Ben's injuries would have on him or his family. He was determined to walk again—to live a normal life again—but if that happened it would be between God and Ben, because doctors didn't know what else to do for him.

"It's something we definitely need to think long and hard about," I said. "But I'm not against it. It'll change our lives and the way we do things. He's still a minor, even though he's in college. He's barely had his license a few months. But he'll be an adult in a couple of years..." I shrugged. "We just have to make sure he doesn't go back to his criminal ways."

"I think Ben keeps a pretty close watch on that aspect of things, though I don't doubt for a minute that Doug does only what he can get away with and that he knows where the loopholes are as far as what he can do with computers. I'm worried about him. He's at a pivotal age, and he needs something more than what he's getting. I don't know what that is, but maybe he just needs someone to love him for who he is right now. There's a lot of pressure on Doug. His mind is a commodity to everyone, including Ben in some respects because there's an expectation that Doug will go right into the FBI academy after college."

"You've thought about this quite a bit," I said, raising a brow.

"I'd never thought about it until Doug mentioned it," Jack said.

I smiled, knowing how Jack's mind worked. He truly was a good man—the best man—and his thoughtfulness and care regarding others never ceased to amaze me. I could be selfish on occasion, living in my own bubble and dealing with my own life, but when I'd married Jack I realized his desires and happiness were more important than my own. And he felt that way about me too. That kind of selflessness was a rare find, especially in marriage, and if Jack felt like Doug belonged with us for the next couple of years then I would happily go along for the ride.

"That means no more sex in the kitchen," I said teasingly. "Or the sunroom, or your office, or the stairs..."

Jack's lips twitched. "He has to leave the house some time, right?"

"We'll make sure of it," I said.

He looked me over from head to toe again and I could tell his mind had shifted to more pleasurable things. "Are you sure we don't have time to go back upstairs?"

"I'll make you a deal," I said. "If we get this case closed today, we can spend the rest of the weekend upstairs."

"Deal," he said immediately. "Let's go talk to Dwight."

We left a note on the fridge for Doug he was bound to see since the probability of him opening the fridge first thing was pretty high, and reminded him to clean up the kitchen after himself, not touch the sword, and to call if there was an emergency.

"This will be a good test to leave him home alone for the day," Jack said.

"What's the test?" I asked. "If the house is still standing he stays?"

"To be fair, your dad set the bar pretty high when it comes to that."

"Touché," I said, getting into the Tahoe.

The phone rang on the way to the station, and Carver's name popped up on the dashboard screen.

Jack hit the accept call button and said, "Carver."

"You sound cranky," Carver said. "Did Jaye make you sleep on the couch?"

"Do I sound cranky?" Jack asked me, turning out of the driveway onto Heresy Road.

"You sound determined," I said supportively. "That's your I'm about to catch a killer voice."

"Oh," Carver said. "Easy mistake. I have to say, we see some unusual stuff when it comes to homicides in D.C. But I've got to hand it to you, that little county of yours takes the cake when it comes to weird. Maybe Michelle and I need to move that direction. I'm getting bored with city crime. It's so yesterday."

Jack raised his brows in surprise. "Do it," Jack said. "It's not a bad commute to the city and the schools are good. We could even be neighbors. You could come over constantly and ask to borrow my tools and never return them."

"Man, you sure do hold a grudge. It was a hammer for Pete's sake. Twelve years ago."

"It matched the set," Jack said.

"I couldn't be your neighbor anyway," Carver said. "You live in the middle of nowhere. Where's the noise and pollution? Where's the Chinese take-out? Where are the cabs?"

"In D.C. where you are," Jack said.

"Exactly my point," Carver said.

"I'm lost," Jack said. "I think I missed your point somewhere along the way."

"I got that military info you needed on David Englander. Always a pleasure digging into Pentagon files. Their security is a mess."

"What'd you find?" Jack asked.

"Nothing special," Carver said. "Good soldier. Follows instructions. No issues with authority. He's got two years left in the reserves, but it looks like he's already been approached for a military job after he finishes his degree. Seems like a good kid."

"That's what I figured it would look like," Jack said. "What about Jaden Matthew's sealed juvie record?"

"Typical stuff," Carver said. "It looks like his family started having financially difficulties. He was enrolled in an elite private school and was removed at fifteen the year before he graduated because they couldn't pay tuition. Ended up in public school and he started hanging with the wrong crowd. Drinking, smoking, joyriding. Stupid kid stuff, and big time rebellion. The kids he was running with decided to rob a convenience store, and Jaden was the driver.

"What he didn't know was one of the kids was armed and a man got shot, so that escalated pretty quickly. They were all caught, but they all swore they didn't know their friend was armed. Jaden was detained for a couple of months and sentenced to mandatory counseling and community service. The judge was lenient and took into consideration the changes that had happened in his life over the past year and that he came from a good home and was an exemplary student. He served his time and fulfilled the punishment and the court determined he was rehabilitated, so they sealed his records on request of his parents and the judge agreed to expunge it so it didn't affect his future. He's had no other issues since then. Looks like he got straightened out."

Jack blew out a breath. "I was really hoping you'd tell me something that made me want to look at one of these kids closer. We've got to narrow down our suspect pool."

"Doug told me what he discovered in the sword," Carver said. "That's how you'll do it. A person who's brilliant enough for science like that isn't going to hide their light under a bushel. They're going to want to show it off. Someone will eventually confess if you keep at it."

"That's what I'm hoping," Jack said. "Jaye and I will come up for a visit when this is over. You can take us to your favorite smog and polluted city restaurant."

"See, when you say it like that it doesn't sound as appealing," Carver said, making me laugh. "But you've got a deal. Now that the FBI knows I'm not functioning from the waist down but that my brain works fine, my work load has increased significantly. Magnolia and I have been working double time. She told me the other day she's starting to feel neglected and that I'm a workaholic."

"Maybe you should buy he a sexy nightie or jewelry to make it up to her," I said.

"Don't encourage him," Jack cut in, giving me a look that made me burst into laughter. "That makes it a thousand times creepier than it already is. Michelle must be the most understanding woman on the planet. Don't forget to schedule time with your actual wife. I'm sure your computer will understand."

"You obviously don't know Magnolia very well," Carver said. "But don't worry. We have a schedule. Magnolia gets Mondays and Thursdays and every other weekend. Michelle gets the rest."

"Oh, good," Jack said. "You've turned into Sister Wives. I don't know how you have time for the High Council after juggling your women."

Carver's gasp was audible. "That no good sneak. Council positions are highly revered and secretive."

"Don't worry. Your secret is safe with us," I said. "Unless we need it for blackmail one day."

"I understand now why you and Michelle get along so well," he said. "It's my curse to have such beautiful and brutal women in my life."

"It's good for you," Jack said. "Changing the subject since I have you on the line, I just got a text from one of my deputies that served a warrant this morning to get the files for Trish Johnson. She's the academic sponsor for the university club and also the event organizer. Apparently, there are some NDAs in her file, which is why the president wouldn't give them to us without a warrant. The warrant was served, but the attorneys are delaying until Monday since it's the weekend and their offices and the university offices are closed. I think they just have something to hide."

"I love it when people have things to hide," Carver said.

"I know you do. Think you can get me whatever it is they're hiding?"

"If I can't I have no business being the head of the High Council," he said.

"And here I thought you would have said you have no business working for the FBI," I told him.

"Most of my black suit colleagues probably say that every day. It's a good thing I'm so useful. And that my security clearance is higher than theirs. I'll get started on this and get it back to you as soon as I can. Peace out."

CHAPTER SIXTEEN

THE TOWNE SQUARE WAS A PRETTY PIECE OF KING George history that managed to unify all four towns that made up the county. Each side of the square was in a different town—King George, Bloody Mary, Newcastle, or Nottingham—and the monstrous Gothic courthouse sat in the middle of the square.

But the street in front of the sheriff's office had been blocked off at each end because of renovation construction, so people had to turn down the side streets to get where they were going. There were plenty of honks and aggravated drivers who didn't like having their routines messed with, even if they had voted to improve the sheriff's office.

There were scaffolds on the sidewalks as they built an extra story on top of the entire building, and the construction crews were working seven days a week to get it done in time, especially since prisoners were having to be moved around while things were being renovated.

Most of the cops found a reason not to sit behind their desk any more than they had to because of the noise, so there wasn't a lot of activity when we walked inside the station. Since it was Saturday, the desk where Jack's secretary sat was empty along with those of a few other administrative personnel, and Sergeant Hill sat behind the enclosed area in the lobby where he manned the entry point.

"Morning, Sheriff," Hill said.

Hill was an older man with bristled gray hair and a wiry mustache who had close to thirty years on the job. He was one of the few who was happy to sit behind a desk and wait for retirement to come, and he had a giant book of crosswords that he worked every day when things were slow. Sometimes he worked them when things *weren't* slow.

"Hill," Jack said. "Who's in?"

"I think Scofield and Jackson are around somewhere, but things got loud with jackhammers a while back, so I couldn't say where they are. I took my hearing aids out half an hour ago."

"Slow night?" Jack asked.

"That's what they tell me," Hill said, filling in squares on the crossword puzzle. "Had a couple of DWIs in King George and an armed robbery in Nottingham. Everyone apprehended. And you've got your wizard murderer in holding, so that makes four overnight guests."

"Not bad for a Friday night," Jack said.

"It's the calm before the storm," Hill said. "Tonight's a full moon. That's when all the crazies come out to play."

"We're going to be in interview for a while," Jack told him. "I'm expecting Martinez with a suspect at some point. Let him know I'm here."

"I'll let him know where you are," Hill said as Jack typed in the code to get into the bullpen.

I waited until we were out of earshot before I asked Jack, "Why do you keep guys like that around to do crosswords on the job?"

"Hill was here long before I got here, and he'll be gone in less than six months. It's not worth the battle to try to get him to do his job after almost thirty years of not doing his job, and you can't fire guys like that. Civil service would hang me out to dry. All I can do is put him in the place he can do the least amount of damage.

"I want my guys who actually work to be the ones out on the streets and taking the risks, because they're the ones paying attention. Besides, if an active threat ever comes in the front door of the sheriff's office, Hill would probably wish he'd paid attention instead of doing his crossword book. So you see, he'll either retire or die, and whichever comes first is really his decision."

"Huh," I said. "You mean you expect people to take personal responsibility for their actions? Maybe you should send the memo to the rest of the country."

Jack snorted and we wound our way through the halls until we reached the hallway that led to the jail. Jack typed in another code on a keypad and the steel door swung open. Dwight was in one of the holding cells, so we didn't have to go through security checkpoints, but I went ahead into Interrogation A and stood against the wall while I waited for Jack to bring him in.

Jack guided Dwight into the room, and he looked much different than he had the last time we'd spoken to him. Gone was the blue makeup and contacts, and in its place was milk-pale skin and freckles. His red hair was gnarled with curls and tangles, and his costume had been replaced with white jail scrubs. He looked impossibly young.

"You remember Dr. Graves?" Jack asked him, leading him to the single metal chair on the far side of the table.

I took a seat across from Dwight, and Jack took the seat next to me.

"Yes," he said, his pale blue eyes somber. "Nice to see you again. You were very kind."

I nodded sympathetically. There was something about this kid that pulled at my heartstrings. I knew he'd killed Kevin. I'd watched the video multiple times. But there was an innocence about Dwight that wasn't like suspects we'd dealt with before, and I was struggling to not go ahead and declare him innocent and be done with it. He'd still taken the life of another human, innocent or not, and the law had to play out here. But I completely understood why the deputies weren't being too strict with him.

"How are you feeling?" I asked. "More in control?"

"Yes," he said, nodding earnestly. "The doctor gave me some stuff to relax and I stopped throwing up, so I figure that's a plus. It's not so bad in here, I guess. My parents came to visit, and all the cops have been really nice." He leaned forward and whispered, as if he was sharing a secret. "Sometimes they'll give me stuff from the vending machines. The food here really sucks."

My mouth twitched at his candidness. "So does the coffee," I said, making him smile for the first time.

"You know why we're here?" Jack asked.

Dwight's smile faded and he nodded. "Kevin."

"That's right," Jack said. "We're trying to find out exactly what happened to Kevin. Maybe what happened in that arena was an accident. Maybe it wasn't. But don't you think Kevin deserves for the truth to come out?"

Dwight had gone even paler and his freckles stood out like tiny beacons on his face, but he nodded in affirmation.

"We talked to the other Kings," Jack said, watching Dwight's reaction.

"They're all jealous," Dwight said. "Kev was the best. No one even came close to getting the kinds of scores he did. Not even me. He was in another league. Totally brilliant."

"If he's so brilliant, why did you get the Archimedes Fellowship?" Jack asked.

"Because the Archimedes Fellowship is only for engineers. Kevin wanted to be a physicist. He got accepted to the Caltech program and was planning to move there this summer. He'd have had his PhD well before his thirtieth birthday."

"That's impressive," Jack said. "But that's a long way from home. What about Madison?"

Dwight snorted. "He wasn't serious about her. She really messed Kev up with that whole video thing. He was so angry. I've never seen anyone that angry. And then he was crazy depressed, and I thought for a while he was going to give up Kaal Dracarian and lay down his axes. He was sleeping all the time, and didn't seem to care about school. I'd try to get him out, but he wouldn't budge from bed, so I'd hang out in his dorm room and play video games and stuff and order pizza. He eventually started eating and commenting on my gaming. And then one day he picked up the controller and it was like things were as they'd always been."

"Sounds like you're a good friend to me," I told him. "People who care about each other or other people don't do the kinds of things those kids did to Kevin."

Dwight's eyes widened and he said, "That's exactly what I told him. When school started back in August and the tournament season began with the new quests, I thought he'd put the whole thing behind him and Kaal was ready to dominate. After he got out of the depression, he started training really hard to improve his skills. He was already dominant, but this put him above and beyond."

"What kind of training?" I asked.

"Different martial arts styles for the most part, but he was taking a boxing class as well so he could move his feet better and faster."

"You never took classes like that?" I asked.

Dwight pinkened slightly. "I've tried a time or two, and it's helped. But I'm kind of a big guy. Brute strength and intimidation works on everyone else but Kevin. I took a fencing class that helped a lot too."

"That's a lot of extra work for a game," Jack said.

Dwight's reaction was the same as if Jack had said a bad word in church. "But it's not just a game. Look at the opportunities, the teaching, the mind expansion. Those quests are not easy. You've got to have a genius-level IQ before you can even hope to make it through. But it also teaches teamwork and camaraderie. And if you do well you're rewarded. It's like the military for smart people."

Jack arched a brow, his look saying everything about Dwight's comment.

"I didn't mean that to come out that way," Dwight said, his face going from pink to scarlet. "There are a lot of smart people in the military. I just mean that none of us are going to be recruited to save the country unless it's with our minds. We know our strengths and weaknesses, and we're not the buffed-up alphas that everyone loves to see as heroes. But by doing this, we get to use our minds and pretend that we're the heroes or villains everyone wants to root for. Sometimes, for people like us, it's easier to live in that world than the real world."

"I understand," Jack said. "I really do. You've got a gift. Don't let people make you feel inferior because they don't understand you or appreciate who you really are."

"Thanks," Dwight said softly.

"How did Madison fit into Kevin's life if he was doing all this new training?" Jack asked.

"I don't know," Dwight said. "It was really weird. I stopped by his dorm one day to play the new *Call of Duty* and she was just there hanging out. It was super awkward because she doesn't know anything about video games, but she was acting all interested and stuff. When she left, I asked him what was going on, and told him after what she'd done to him he should never look at her face again, but he said he had everything under control and that he was going to enjoy her company while it lasted."

Dwight's face went red again and he pressed his lips together.

"What?" Jack asked.

"Umm...well, Kevin said he didn't want to spend his whole life a virgin, and that if she wanted to apologize by having sex with him then he wasn't going to stop her. I kind of understood what he was going for at that point, but I told him I didn't think it was nice to use a person that way. But he said I didn't understand. She'd used him and he was using her. It was mutual using. So I dropped it after that. But it was like he really didn't like her at all."

The look on Dwight's face was a mixture of apologetic and confused. "Like, he despised her. Why would you spend so much time with a person you felt that way about? How could he have sex with her if he hated her?"

"Kevin was hurt," I said. "Deep-down hurt. People do a lot of crazy things when the hurt runs that deep."

"I guess so," Dwight said. "I don't know why she stuck around because he was rude to her and kind of demeaning, but she'd get upset and then he'd do something nice for her like buy her jewelry or write a paper for her. It was messed up in the head."

"So Kevin wouldn't have thought about taking her with him to Caltech?" Jack asked.

"No way," Dwight said, shaking his head. "He told me before the Christmas break he was going to break it off because he had to focus on the tournament. He said more than one man had been ruined by sex, and he wasn't going to allow himself to be another. It was time to get his act together and be the Kaal Dracarian that would go down in history. The Kaal that everyone would know was the greatest."

"Why does that make you sound so sad?" I asked.

"Because it is kind of sad," he answered. "Whatever happened to Kevin after that video went viral, it really changed him. And then when I thought he was finally coming back around he and Madison started hooking up, and he turned into this completely different person. It's like he decided he didn't want to be Kevin anymore and he started taking on the persona of Kaal Dracarian full time.

"Kaal is a leader—a warrior—and he takes no prisoners. He's rough and crude, but charming and charismatic in a way that makes people love him. Kevin started to behave that way. It's the only reason I could think of that a girl who looks like Madison would be remotely interested in someone like Kevin. But it really just turned him into a jerk."

"You and Kevin were friends," I said, more as a statement than a question. "You were closer to him than anyone else in the group."

"I told you before," he said. "He was my best friend. He wasn't the easiest guy to be friends with. Self-absorbed and socially awkward. But I think we were friends because we weren't direct competitors. I knew I'd never catch up to Kevin's score, and I was fine with that. It's not like you can do this stuff forever or make a living, right? I knew the time would come to an end. But I don't think the others see it that way. We're all friends, I guess. You can't help but be when you spend that many hours together, sharing ideas and working through the science. It's nice to be around people who aren't stupid. I think that's the biggest reason the Kings hung out all the time. It's hard to feel normal when you're the smartest person in the room."

"Was Madison smart enough to rework your sword and turn it into a weapon that could kill?"

"No way," Dwight said, shaking his head. "She's kind of an idiot. Kevin tutored her for a while before the whole video thing, and he always came back saying it was a good thing she had her looks to fall back on. Kevin even suggested to her once that she should get her teaching certification instead of trying to get into grad school. I think she got offended because she cancelled their next couple of tutoring sessions. Kevin has never been good at reading human emotion. He was kind of a robot when it came to stuff like that. At least before he turned into Kaal."

"And you?" Jack asked.

"Oh, I'm socially awkward too," Dwight said, a hint of a grin on his mouth. "Just in a different way."

"I meant are you good at reading human emotions," Jack corrected.

"Oh," Dwight said, flushing. "Better than Kevin. I mean, I at least notice if the words coming out of my mouth are making a person feel like junk. But Kevin is usually oblivious. He's very black and white. He just says whatever comes to mind and doesn't care about the consequences." He stopped and corrected himself. "*Didn't* care about the consequences. I keep forgetting he's not here. But I can't forget either because I saw him die."

"It's okay," I said. "What do you mean he didn't care about the consequences?"

"This one time during a Kings meeting, Dr. Johnson was talking about a theory from her dissertation and Kevin called it moronic. Boy, was she mad. I told him later he was lucky he didn't have her for a professor anymore. She would've failed him just on principle. Just things like that. To him he wasn't being disrespectful to a professor. He was just being honest. And science has to be about the truth."

Jack leaned back in the chair and studied Dwight for a couple of minutes, his dark eyes searching, but I didn't know what for.

"I should have come to you for intimidation tips," Dwight said. "You're really good at it. And I appreciate your line of questioning. It's very thorough. You add a lot of psychology into your techniques. Is that your background?"

Jack full-out smiled, and it caught Dwight off guard because he sat up in his chair a little straighter.

"You're a smart kid," Jack said. "Let's just say that my background is varied and my experience has been useful. I didn't learn everything in grad school."

"You went to grad school?" Dwight asked, respect in his gaze. "I mean, she's a doctor so I know where she stands on the education spectrum. But it's good to know you're an academic as well. People don't put enough store in education these days."

"There are all kinds of educations," Jack said. "Some of the stupidest people I've ever met talk about their multiple degrees. Here's a life tip, never set your level of expectation based on someone's education. It's not my advanced degrees that make me a good cop. That stuff makes me a good administrator. But the time I've spent on the streets learning human nature, the times I've put on body armor and risked my life to save someone else, and the time I've spent dissecting every ounce of evidence to bring justice to victims is what makes me a good cop."

I could tell Dwight was soaking in Jack's words like he was hearing from God himself. He'd probably not had a lot of men like Jack bother to show any interest in him.

"I understand what you're saying," Dwight said. "And I'll remember your advice for the future. Thank you."

Jack's lip quirked at the formality of Dwight's appreciation, and he said, "You're welcome."

"You're going to want to know about the sword next," Dwight said. "That's the next logical line of questioning."

"That's an excellent observation," Jack said. "Maybe you'd make a good investigator."

Dwight pursed his lips tightly and shook his head. "No, I don't think so. I'd like to make money."

"Tell me about the sword," Jack said. "How did you build it? What are its functions?"

"It's called Dybbuk," Dwight said. "It's the legendary sword of Lord Uridak. He's the elvish leader of the Sheol Realm. In the Hebrew Bible, the

Sheol is a place of darkness where the dead go. And Dybbuk is the malicious soul of a dead person that invades someone who is living. I created an entire world based on Uridak. There's even fan fiction written about him."

"So essentially," Jack said, "you're the bad guy?"

"In a sense," Dwight said, grinning. "It's much more fun to play the bad guy. But every character who competes in the quests and tournament can choose a path of good or evil. I have almost as many followers as Kaal Dracarian does. People like a bad guy they can love to hate."

"How long have you been Lord Uridak?" Jack asked.

"I created the character my freshman year of high school," Dwight said. "I've spent years developing the character and the world he belongs in. I have maps and models of the Sheol Realm I made from scratch. Uridak has always been a sword wielder, but he's also proficient in magic. In my stories Dybbuk is a magical sword that shoots lightning."

"It's always been that way?" Jack asked. "That's a fact everyone would know?"

"Of course," Dwight said. "It's been that way from the beginning. Though when I first started out all I could afford were plastic swords or ones I made myself. I was finally able to save up enough to have one made to my specifications. It cost me almost a thousand bucks."

"That's a lot of money," Jack said. "Especially for a high school student."

Dwight's lips twitched. "To be honest, the summer after my freshman year I got grounded and my mom took my phone and game systems away. All we had was this old computer, but I was able to get online. It turns out I was pretty good at online poker, so I won enough money to invest in Uridak so he could be everything I saw in my head.

"I found a welder to make the sword. It's not made of iron or steel. Those metals are too heavy. It's a magnesium-based alloy, so it's very light, but very strong. The only problem was I need the sword to be hollow on the inside so I could add the magical components. You get flair points from the judges for enhancing your weapons or costumes.

"So I drew out the iconic zigzag design that Uridak is famous for, and the welder put the pieces together on an interior hinge so you can't tell that it's two pieces from the outside. On the other side is an interior spring latch, so all I have to do is press down in the right place and the sword pops open."

"We watched some of your previous tournament videos. In one the whole sword was lit up with a yellow light so it looked like it glowed, and in other videos sparks could be seen shooting out the end of the sword."

"Sure," Dwight said. "Flair points for extra effects. I ran tube lighting on the inside to get the yellow glow, but it made the metal hot to the touch, so I eventually took it out. The sparks were made from wires hooked up to a battery. I was able to finesse it some to eventually make an electrical arc. But it was only impressive visually if my opponent was wearing metal armor. When I brought the sword in range an electrical arc would appear and connect with the metal on the costume. It was pretty cool. Since the tube lights didn't work, I tampered with the metal some, soldering tiny blue lights along the blade to make it look like the electricity was traveling down the entire length of the sword and arcing onto my opponent."

"That's interesting," Jack said. "What about the hologram? When did you add that?"

Dwight's mouth stopped moving and seemed to be stuck in the *O* position. "I...I don't understand."

"I think you do," Jack said. "When you turned Dybbuk on, you had to realize those weren't the modifications you'd made. A hologram is pretty advanced. Unless your skills improved greatly from the last tournament to this one, you didn't make those modifications. Or maybe someone helped you?"

"No," he said. "I didn't make them."

"And when you turned the sword on you didn't stop to think what was happening?" Jack asked. "It didn't cross your mind to stop the tournament and let someone know that wasn't your sword?"

"Everything is a blur when you're up there. All the bright lights and smoke around the ring for effect." He shrugged. "You get lost in the moment and the character. And when I turned that sword on and the blue flame rippled down the metal I just thought that maybe the magic finally worked. I know it's childish. But it's true."

"Holograms aren't exactly easy to come by," Jack said. "It's complicated science and it can get expensive. Who do you know who works with holograms?"

He licked his lips nervously, but he kept eye contact. "I don't know anyone who would enhance my sword like that. Why would they try to make it better? It's a competition."

"Come on, Dwight," Jack said. "Out of your entire group of super nerds, not one of you has an interest in holograms? I find that kind of hard to believe."

"Of course we have an interest in holograms," he said. "It's a fascinating science. Even Dr. Johnson's field of study encompasses holograms. But KGU killed the program a long time ago, so it's all just theory when we talk about it. We don't have the equipment or experience to do much more than that."

"Trish Johnson has experience with hologram technology?" Jack asked, leaning forward.

"Yeah, I mean, she's an optical engineer. That's what they do. But she couldn't get the university to reinstate the program so she said she decided to teach history instead. But we talk about a lot of different theories among the Kings. We're all scientists with varied interests. It's the science that keeps us together."

"If you say that you didn't make the holographic effects on your sword," Jack said, "then that means someone else tampered with it. Who had access?"

"It's not like it's locked in a vault or anything," Dwight said. "I keep it in a glass case in my apartment for the most part. But sometimes I'll bring it to meetings, and I'll bring it along if we do a low-key D&D game on the weekend or something. But we mostly do those at my place since I've got more room. Everyone brings their weapons, costumes, and dice. That's part of the game."

"You never turned the sword on before you stepped foot in the arena to fight Kevin?" I asked. "You didn't check to see if it worked or to play with it a little?"

Sweat dotted Dwight's upper lip. "I didn't really have time," he explained. "You see, I had the stomach flu for most of last week, so I went home and stayed with my mom for a few days so she could take care of me. She wanted me to pull out of the tournament altogether, but I knew I couldn't do that. I had to fight no matter what or I'd be disqualified for the rest of the season.

"I could barely get out of bed the day of the tournament," he said. "But I felt a little better after I showered and had some soup. I think that's why I threw up the last time we talked. Sorry about that."

"We've had worse," I told him. "How'd you get everything ready for the tournament? If you had the sword and your costume, then that only leaves you who could have tampered with the sword."

He was already shaking his head no. "That's what I'm trying to tell you. I was too sick to get my stuff and bring it with me. She could barely get me to the car. I was in bed solid from Sunday to Thursday morning. My mom was able to do my makeup at home since my old makeup case was there, and then she drove me to the arena and dropped me off. I made sure everything was there and waiting for me so I could just get dressed and go on stage. I didn't really have time to check anything before I walked on. I literally limped out of the car, got dressed, and walked into the ring to fight."

"Who brought your things to the arena and made sure they were in your dressing room?" Jack asked.

Dwight wiped at his upper lip and went white, and I wondered if he was going to throw up again. Jack must have had the same thought because he leaned back from the table.

"If you didn't mean to kill Kevin on purpose, then you've got to help us find out who did," Jack said. "Who put your things in your dressing room?"

"Kevin did," he said.

CHAPTER SEVENTEEN

"KEVIN WAS IN POSSESSION OF YOUR SWORD?" I asked. "You let your opponent handle your equipment?"

"I mean, he's my best friend," Dwight said. "I told you it wasn't like that between us. He wouldn't have damaged it. There's an honor code between the Kings."

"When did you know Kevin would be the one you were fighting in the tournament?" I asked.

"The lottery is drawn forty-eight hours before the tournament starts so we all have time to study our opponents and decide on a strategy. There are forty competitors still left in the quest who qualified for this tournament. So when paired off, that's twenty fights. It kind of sucks to draw someone from your own school because you want your whole team to improve in the rankings, but there's no rule against it. Kev and I were randomly selected to fight each other and so were Midnight and Thunderclap."

Dwight's voice got soft and confusion flickered in his eyes. "I just don't understand it. Kev and I have fought loads of times before, and I always lose. I didn't expect to win, especially feeling the way I was. His axes are super light, and the martial arts classes made him almost impossible to score points against. He just moved so fast.

"The only reason I fight as well as I do against Kev is because we practice together and I study his movements and patterns, so I've at least learned defenses and effective blocks against him. It's certainly made our fighting more entertaining, and it lasts longer than when he fights other opponents. That's why they had us fighting last. They knew we'd be the big draw of the tournament. But I didn't know...didn't know what would happen to Kev."

"Was your sword in your apartment before Kevin got it for the tournament?" Jack asked.

"Yes, it was in the glass case, and my costume was all together so all he had to do was pick them up. I put an extra key under the mat so he could get in."

"So someone accessed your apartment after you left to go to your mom's and before Kevin came to get the sword for the tournament. That's a very short window of time. Who could add the hologram to your sword in that amount of time? You know what I think, Dwight?" Jack asked.

Dwight shook his head and said, "No," but the word was barely audible.

"I think you know who did it," Jack said. "I think you all know who did it, but you're not saying anything. An honor code, right? That hologram is a calling card. It's special. And not everyone can do it. So who was it?"

We left Dwight Parr in holding, and went back to Jack's office. Martinez had come in with Chad Wheeler and put him in one of the conference rooms, and Durrant had come back after trying to serve the warrant to get Trish Johnson's files.

"I want someone to bring her in," Jack told Martinez. "You can put her in an interrogation room until we get to her. I'm waiting to get some more information, and I don't care if she has to sit and wait on us a while. She could've told us she knew the sword had that hologram calling card. And she could've told us she had experience with holograms. Now it just makes me think she was trying to cover something up."

"There's no such things as coincidences, right, boss?" Martinez asked.

"That's what I've heard," Jack said. "Who else is on duty today?"

"Colburn is the LT on duty," Durrant said. "And Wachowski, Hops, Riley, and Walters are on patrol."

"Good," Jack said. "Send Hops to my house to retrieve Doug and the sword. Tell her to glove up. I want prints dusted on the inside of the sword. Let's see if whoever left their calling card left evidence behind. Several sets of prints were taken from Dwight Parr's place. We can see if there are any matches.

"I want you and Wachowski and Riley to go round up the rest of the Kings and Madison Marbury and bring them in. Everyone is covering for someone, and they know that the worst Dwight could get charged with is manslaughter two, but they're probably feeling pretty confident we'll rule it as an accident and not charge him at all. There's just no evidence to say he did it maliciously and intentionally, especially if his alibi holds up with his mom and the stomach flu.

"And with the victim being the last one to touch the sword before Dwight, that gives us even less reason to hold him past seventy-two hours. But at the core, the Kings are a secret society, even within the bigger community of the club organization. They meet in a secret location behind locked doors. They might have inner squabblings or jealousy, but at the end of the day they're a part of something that only a few elites get to belong to. In their mind, it's a society worth protecting and preserving, no matter the cost. It's no different than any other secret society. It's just finding the weak link in the chain."

"I'm on it," Durrant said.

"Oh, and let your LT know," Jack said. "I'm sure he'll want in on the fun."

"I don't doubt it, sir," Durrant said, and then he and Martinez left to go ruin several people's days.

"If you think the killer is one of the Kings," I said, "why are we wasting our time with Chad?"

"A couple of reasons," Jack said, opening his office door and going inside. I followed behind him and sat in the chair across from his desk. "The first is that he has motive, especially if Madison told him Kevin was out for revenge. The second is that I just don't like what he did and he got off right after the stunt he pulled with Kevin. We'll question him and cross all our t's and dot our i's."

"And Madison?" I asked, wondering what Jack had planned. I could tell his mind was running a hundred miles a minute, and something had clicked when we'd been talking to Dwight.

"I want to see her reactions," Jack said. "She's the root cause of the trouble. And I'm not entirely convinced she doesn't know something. This is a group of kids that seems to thrive on drama. Why not give it to them?"

"You're very sexy when you solve crimes," I said. "Do you know that?"

"Of course," he said, looking down at his phone, but I could see the smile on his lips. "I know my brain turns you on. And I like it when you're turned on. And you made a deal. You said if we solve the case today we'll spend the rest of the weekend in bed. I'm very motivated."

"Hmm," I said. "It sounds like I should get more anti-inflammatories."

"It wouldn't hurt," Jack said. He read a text and then typed a quick reply. "Carver was able to find the court documents pertaining to Trish Johnson. He's sending them over now. We have a warrant so we're covered, even though the courts are closed today. I'll bet you a thousand dollars she walks in with that jerk-off attorney."

"That's a sucker's bet," I said. "You think she's in on it?"

"I think they're all in on it," he said. "I just don't know to what extent. I don't like being lied to, even by omission. And every time we've talked to any of them I know they've been withholding information. You could tell they'd already discussed how much and what they would say when we stepped into their box theater. Every time we talk to one of them, we find out something a little more and have to keep going back to the drawing board. And Trish is their leader. She's an optical engineer. And she's got a sealed file protected by a whole bunch of NDAs. Which Jim Coleman damn well knows doesn't mean anything in a murder investigation. But he made me jump through the hoops anyway.

"Then you have Madison and Chad, who obviously belong together, because they're both pretty awful people. She's got every reason to want Kevin dead, and we'll know soon what Chad's thoughts are about Kevin's idea for revenge. But if Madison was behind it she'd need a partner to work the science. That's not her strength.

"Oddly enough, even though Dwight Parr dealt the final blow, he's the most innocent one among them." He stopped and looked at his watch, and then checked his email, pulling up the information on Trish Johnson that Carver had sent over.

I could tell Jack was ticked, and he rarely let his aggravation show. But this was the kind of case where the body didn't reveal a lot. It didn't lead to specific clues and there was no DNA or anything in the tox screen that could lead us to a killer. We were following the motive trail, and that's really all we could do. But if a bunch of genius-level kids thought they were going to get away with murder and run the cops in circles, then Jack was about to lay the hammer down.

The printer started to whirr, but Jack's eyes hadn't left the screen where he was skimming the court documents on Trish Johnson.

"What is it?" I asked.

"It looks like Trish is going to have some explaining to do," Jack said.

I decided to lay off the coffee for a little while and switched to soda, and I took something for my knee while I had the chance. Sitting for so long while we talked to Dwight had made it stiffen again, but my adrenaline was surging because I knew we were on the right track to solving Kevin's murder, and that was enough to keep my mind off the pain in my body.

"Ready?" Jack asked after we'd made Chad wait for a good forty-five minutes in the tiny interrogation room.

"When you are," I said.

"Do you have more skirts like that?"

"I don't think so," I said. "Why?"

"It presents an excellent view from the back. Buy more of them. A lot more."

I grinned and said, "You've got a one-track mind today."

"Not true," he said. "It's very distinctly two-tracked. Solve murder. Make love to my very sexy wife." He stopped at the door of the interrogation room and said, "Put on your mean face." And then he opened the door.

I recognized Chad from the infamous video, but he was even smarmier in person. He was every stereotypical frat boy picture I could conjure, with his spiked blond hair and angular jaw. He had the collar of his baby-blue polo shirt flipped up and the sleeves were tight around his muscled biceps.

"Chad Wheeler," Jack said. "We've been looking for you."

"Looks like you found me," he said, smirking. "How long is this going to take? I've got plans today."

Jack gave him a wolf's smile, and Chad's smirk

faded some. "We talked to Madison yesterday," Jack said.

"So what?" Chad asked.

"Well, I don't know if you've heard, but Kevin Schwartzman was murdered a couple of days ago."

"Who?" Chad asked, rolling his eyes.

"You're not going to want to start down this path with me, Chad," Jack said, leaning on the table that divided them. "Punks like you are a dime a dozen. And you may think you're the big man on campus, but here, you're nobody. And I can make sure you stay nobody. So I'm going to say his name again, and you're going to stop bullshitting me—Kevin Schwartzman."

Chad rolled his eyes and crossed his arms over his chest. "Yeah, yeah," he said. "I know who he is."

"Good," Jack said. "The truth is going to work well in this situation. You and Kevin don't exactly have the best history. You lost your scholarship and got kicked out of your fraternity because of what you and Madison and your buddies did to him."

Chad shifted in his chair. "Madison didn't have anything to do with that."

"Still lying for her?" Jack asked. "She told us yesterday how he'd gotten his revenge and that he had plans for you too. What did he have planned for you?"

"Who knows?" Chad said. "But I was ready for him. A little creep like Kevin isn't going to get the best of me. He deserved what he got. He destroyed Madison's whole future, and I'm sure he would've tried to do the same to mine. More than he already had."

"Just so we're clear," Jack said. "You realize it all could've been avoided if you'd not done what you did in the first place, right? You're not a victim here."

"Whatever you say, man," he said. "But Madison didn't deserve that."

"You must really love Madison," Jack said.

"Sure," he said. "We've been through a lot together."

"You love her enough to help her kill Kevin? Because I've got to say, as far as motives go, I've never seen a better one for killing someone."

"This is stupid," Chad said. "Everyone knows it was that fat guy Dwight who killed him. It was televised. It's all over the internet. You can't pin a murder on me or Madison. I don't even know why I'm here."

"You're an engineering major, right, Chad?" Jack asked.

"So?"

"So someone turned Dwight's sword into a high-voltage cattle prod, and when it touched Kevin's armor it cooked him to death. That seems like something an electrical engineering student might know how to do."

"So what?" he asked. "There are probably a thousand engineering students. Go interview all of them."

"What about holograms?" Jack asked, "You ever

have an interest in holograms? Maybe back when Dr. Johnson was teaching in the engineering department."

"Sure," he said. "It was cool, but the program got shut down."

"You ever meet with Dr. Johnson now?"

"I had her for a history class last year," he said. "It was kind of weird. But we're not hooking up if that's what you're asking."

"It's funny, because you run in the same circles as Kevin," Jack said. "Every bit of evidence in this case could lead back to you in some way. You and Madison pretty much destroyed Kevin's life. He starts dating your ex-girlfriend. He breaks up with her with ultimate revenge in mind. You're an engineering major just like Dwight, so you'd be knowledgeable to make changes to Dwight's sword and cause him to kill the person who's making your and Madison's life so difficult. Madison warned you that Kevin would be planning his own revenge against you. And you've got experience with holograms. That's a lot more than just a coincidence when you're talking about murder."

"Look," Chad said. "I didn't kill Kevin. I'm not really sorry he's dead, but I didn't do it. Can I go home now?"

"No," Jack said. "I don't think so. Have you ever been to Dwight's apartment?"

Chad scoffed. "Of course not. Why would I go there?"

"I'm going to need you to give me an alibi for

Tuesday, Wednesday, and Thursday of this last week."

"How am I supposed to know?" he asked. "That was days ago. I went to class. I went home. I had a couple of beers at Beefcakes and played some pool."

"Isn't Beefcakes over by the Korean barbecue restaurant off campus?" Jack asked.

"Yeah, so?"

"That's where Dwight's apartment is," Jack said. "So I'm going to ask you again before we take your prints and start matching them. Have you ever been to Dwight's apartment?"

CHAPTER EIGHTEEN

WE LEFT CHAD ALONE IN THE INTERROGATION ROOM with a pen and a piece of paper so he could write down a detailed list of what his days and nights looked like earlier in the week.

"Sheriff," Martinez said, catching us on the way to pay a visit with Trish Johnson, who'd been waiting in another interrogation room. "The kids are starting to arrive. We're still waiting on Wachowski to show up with Madison Marbury, and Hops and Doug just showed up with the sword."

"Get prints from the inside of the sword, and have Doug help take apart the hilt or anything else that might have prints. And then ask Doug to reassemble the sword. You've all got about an hour, so not much time. And then I want everyone in the conference room for a little show-and-tell."

"Do you want us to keep the kids separated until you're ready for them?" Martinez asked.

"No, put them all in the largest conference

room together," Jack said. "But have Hops stand guard inside the room. I don't want them to have a chance to get their stories straight. And she's a good observer. She'll pick it up if any of them start to sweat."

"Got it, boss," Martinez said, and headed back down the hallway to the bullpen.

"You think Doug can put that sword back together and workable in less than an hour?" I asked.

"Yep," he said. "As smart as those kids are, none of them are Doug. I guarantee he learned everything he wanted to know about holograms the second he took it apart, and he can put it back together in his sleep. Let's go pay a visit to Trish Johnson. All roads keep leading back to her, so I'm really interested what she's got to say about all this."

"You know what this case reminds me of?" I asked.

"What?"

"When we worked the murder that involved the Aryan Nation," I said. "Secret societies and everyone covering for each other, providing alibis or muddying the water with half-truths. Parents have sent their kids off to college to get an education so they can go out into the world and be productive. But what are these kids really learning? That they're elite? That they're untouchable because they're so smart? That right and wrong are a blurred line, and they can walk in shades of gray as long as they stick together?"

"This is an age where mentors play a huge role in shaping thoughts and minds, and all these kids have is Trish Johnson. If the mentor is corrupt, guess what the seeds will be? But look at someone like Doug. He's got Carver and us. And we're helping to build him as a person. Not just a genius whose only function is to be brilliant all the time."

I put my hand on Jack's arm, stopping him before we went in to talk to Trish Johnson. "You're going to make an amazing father one day. Really," I said. "Any kid who gets you in their life is privileged beyond all measure."

I could tell the words meant a lot to him, especially because Jack had a son out there somewhere who he'd never met and probably never would meet, and that child was missing out on a great opportunity. All I could do was hope that the father in Jack's son's life was as amazing as Jack.

Emotion filled his gaze and he leaned down to kiss me softly. "Thank you," he whispered. "Now put your mean face on again."

Jack opened the door, and I walked into the room ahead of him. I couldn't keep the surprise off my face. "Looks like I should've taken that bet after all," I told Jack.

"Where's your fancy attorney?" he asked Trish.

"He's the university's attorney," she said, icily. She was dressed much like the first time we met her, in jeans and a KGU sweatshirt, and her long dark hair was in a messy knot on top of her head. "I'd prefer not to have to call him in unless I have to. I live on a teacher's salary."

"Good," Jack said. "Then we can make this short and sweet. I'm going to give you the opportunity to come clean with me. Things aren't going to be good for you if you don't. Start talking."

Jack tossed the file onto the table that held the printed court papers Carver had sent over, and she looked at them curiously before meeting Jack's gaze again. She wasn't the least bit afraid or intimidated by Jack's threat.

"I'm here to cooperate," she said. "If you're going to deliver threats then I'm happy to call in the expensive attorney."

"If you don't start talking I'm going to charge you for murder and keep you behind bars for the next seventy-two hours until your attorney can work his magic," Jack said. "It's the weekend, you know, and I don't think it's the kind of accommodations you're used to. You know exactly why you're here. So start talking."

She glared daggers at Jack for so long I wondered if she was going to speak. And Jack had obviously had enough because he moved to open the door and leave.

"Fine," she said. "But I'm not sure exactly what I'm supposed to tell you."

"Think hard," Jack said. "I'm sure something relevant to the murder of a twenty-one-year-old student who was struck by a sword with a very realistic hologram and electrocuted by a souped-up cattle prod will come to mind."

She nodded and said, "So I'm guessing you know my experience with holograms."

Jack put his finger on the file folder. "NDAs don't count in a murder investigation."

She nodded and seemed to deflate some. "When I first started at the university seventeen years ago, I was brought on as an assistant professor for the engineering department. My specialty is optical engineering, but optical engineers also work closely with the physics department in the study and creation of holograms.

"Eventually I worked my way toward tenure and became the head of the department," she said. "My research was being published, and the program was doing well. But it's an expensive program. Our budget was in the millions of dollars every year, and it's still considered somewhat of an experimental science. But we were making breakthroughs. And then I published a paper with groundbreaking research."

She stopped talking and stared off in the distance sullenly, her arms crossed under her breasts.

"Except the paper you published wasn't your work, was it?" Jack asked. "It was a physics student who'd come up with the groundbreaking research, and someone else recognized that the work you published seemed very familiar. But you're a calculating woman, aren't you? You thought if you paid the student back by having sex with him that all would be forgiven and forgotten."

"He's an adult," she said, angrily. "Not a minor. And who I have sex with is no one's business but my own. It was a mistake, okay? And I've paid the price for it."

"What happened?" Jack asked her.

She sighed, swinging the foot of her crossed leg. "I was very comfortable in my position. And I'm a good teacher. KGU had become one of the most sought-after science schools because of our faculty and research reputations. We were competing with the big schools like Caltech and MIT, and our grants and funding were growing. Then David came in."

"David Englander?" Jack asked.

"Yes," she said. "He came in from the military, and he wasn't like my normal students. He was a man. Not only a man, but a man with a mind—a brilliant mind. I'd always focused on my career, so I never really had many relationships, and David was convenient. At least at first. I knew the military was sending him to school for a very specific purpose. They have a job waiting for him when he graduates. He can't even tell me what it is because it's top secret.

"Anyway, things heated up quick, and then we started staying late in the lab working on special projects and just having fun. And he comes to me one day with a formula and a drawing, and it was like being punched in the gut. He'd figured it out before I had. But he was just a student, and I could get it published in an academic journal where he couldn't. So I submitted it."

"Was he angry?" Jack asked.

"Despite what you think you know from those court documents," she said. "David and I have a mature relationship. I told him that I submitted the work, and we talked it through. I gave him credit in the publication, but I told him that without a respected academic like me behind the work he would've never been able to break into the academic world until he could get his doctorate. He agreed. And we decided to keep working together on future projects. It wasn't a big deal."

"Except that Kevin made it a big deal," Jack said. "Right?"

She blew out a slow breath. "Kevin thought he was doing the right thing," she said. "He was just a freshman at the time, and David and I have both forgiven and forgotten."

"Kevin turned you in?" I asked.

"Kevin was there when David worked out the formula, so he knew it wasn't mine. Kevin had an interest in optical engineering and the hologram department, so he was always hanging around and paying attention to what was going on. I think at the time Kevin was jealous because David and I were spending so much time together, and as a result of that David progressed quite a bit faster than Kevin. Kevin wasn't used to having anyone be better at him in anything. Kevin is—

was—the most brilliant and gifted student I've ever taught. If the program was still around I know he could have made his own academic breakthroughs."

"Let me guess, Kevin wasn't satisfied with David advancing past him or getting the credit in the academic journal, so he decided to kill two birds with one stone."

"Bingo," she said. "He turned me in to the university and wrote a letter to the publication so it was pulled while there was a pending investigation. And then during the investigation it came out about my relationship with David. It's against policy to have a relationship with a student in your own department. And while the article was pulled, another professor from MIT submitted a similar paper with slight tweaks to what we'd done, and he got all the credit."

"So you just gave up teaching what you loved and moved to a different department?" Jack asked.

"Technically, I was asked to leave the university altogether," she said. "But I'm tenured, and nothing I did was technically illegal. Just unethical. So I declined the invitation to find another university, and I chose to move laterally to the history department since I'm qualified there as well. The things we do for love, right?"

"You and David still have a relationship?" I asked.

Her black eyes lasered on mine. "Don't look at me with judgment," she snapped.

"We're asking questions," I said. "It's our job to find a murderer. Someone else can judge."

"You think I haven't heard it all over the last few years?" she asked. "David came in as a twenty-one-year-old freshman. He's twenty-five now, and there's twenty years between us. But I don't care. It's not the university's place or your place to worry about my private life."

"It's our place only when it pertains to murder," Jack said. "We don't care what you do in your private life. It sounds to me like you're the one who has a problem with it."

"You've admitted that you and David have experience with holograms," I said, breaking in before she could start another tirade. "So advanced that you developed something no one had ever seen before. Dwight Parr had the stomach flu all last week. He didn't arrive at the arena until just before his fight. But you knew that, right? You're the coordinator of the entire event. Which means you also knew that Dwight's sword had been left unattended for a few days before the tournament. Plenty of time to tweak it so Dwight would be the one to kill Kevin. The hologram that appeared on Dwight's sword was something of a calling card. A way for the killer to show off their skills."

Trish looked at me head-on, but there was worry in the depths of her dark eyes.

"Did you make sure that the lottery picked Dwight and Kevin to fight each other?" Jack asked

"No, of course not," she said. "It's a computer

program that makes the selections. I don't know what happened with Kevin. I watched it in real time just like everyone else. And it was the most horrible thing I've ever seen."

"Maybe you think that's a fitting punishment for someone who almost ruined your life," Jack said. "Almost ruined your relationship with David."

"No, I told you," she said. "David and I have both put it behind us. We saw Kevin every day for the past three years at Kings meetings. There was no bad blood between any of us. It's science. We all want the best for the science community, and within that structure we're a tight unit."

"Tight enough to lie for each other?" Jack asked. "Tight enough to cover for each other? That was something you had the opportunity to teach when Kevin and David and the others became Kings, right? If Kevin had known the rules—if he'd kept his mouth shut—then none of this would have happened to you. So you molded them all. Taught them how to keep secrets. How to cover for each other. And you taught them things in that black box theater they weren't getting in any classroom. Were you proud when you saw that hologram erupt from Dwight's sword? Even at the expense of Kevin, was the science more important? Is that what you've taught them? Dwight might have wielded the sword, but your hands have blood on them."

"I didn't kill Kevin," she said.

"I guess it makes all of you feel better to be able to say that since you weren't holding the weapon.

I've sat across from a lot of criminals," Jack said. "They were sitting right where you are. But I have to tell you, Dr. Johnson. You're a pretty terrible person. And you've created a lot of other terrible people. If I could lock you away forever for that alone, I'd do it."

CHAPTER NINETEEN

By the time we came out of the interview room with Trish the hour we'd given Doug and the fingerprint team was more than used up.

"Tell me you've got news, Martinez," Jack said, coming into the bullpen.

"You're not going to believe this one," Martinez said, handing over the report.

"I think I am," Jack said.

"You knew it was him," Martinez said, shocked. "How'd you know?"

"Because people can never keep secrets as well as they think they can," Jack said. "Their own interests or egos always get in the way."

I'd caught on to the conclusion Jack was coming to while we'd been talking to Trish Johnson, and I hadn't had a chance to ask Jack how long he'd suspected. But when I looked at the fingerprint analysis, there was only one explanation—only one person responsible for the death of Kevin Schwartzman.

"Tell the guys who've been helping with this case to come into the conference room and form a perimeter," Jack said. "They want a show, then we'll give them one."

I could see the large conference room from where we stood and the grouping of people inside of it who sat around the long wooden table. Miley, Savannah, Jaden, Nikhil, and David sat close at one end of the table. And Madison Marbury sat at the other end alone, ignoring the others and looking at her phone.

I watched with curiosity as Chad was brought in by one of the deputies, and he took a seat next to Madison. They looked at each other briefly, and then Madison went back to her phone. But Chad eyed the others at the end of the table.

And then Dwight was brought in from holding in handcuffs and his white scrubs, and there seemed to be a collective intake of breath as he was led to a chair right in the middle of the table. He didn't make eye contact with any of them, but stared at his cuffed hands.

It wasn't long before the door opened again and Trish Johnson was led inside. Everyone stared at her as she entered, and she smiled and spoke to them as if they were having a day at the park instead of sitting in a police station. She even went so far as to give Dwight a one-armed hug around his shoulders before she took the seat that put her between him and David. Now that she and David were sitting next to each other, the intimacy they shared was obvious, just in a casual look or the way they both slipped their hands under the table at the same time for a quick touch.

"She's a piece of work, isn't she?" I asked Jack.

"That's one word for it," he said. "Look at her talking to Chad and Madison. She knows them. And not just in an *I've seen you around campus* or *taught you in a couple of classes*. Every one of them are connected."

"Let's go disconnect them," I said.

"Where's Doug?" Jack asked Martinez.

"He's in your office with the sword. Want me to get him?"

"Yes," Jack said. "And we're still missing one person. He should be here any second." Then he looked at me and said, "That was the phone call I had to make. Someone needs to take responsibility."

At that moment, Jim Coleman walked into the sheriff's office and looked around, his eyes meeting with Jack's through the plexiglass partition where Sergeant Hill guarded the entrance.

Jack came to open the door for him and let him through.

"Jack," Jim said, shaking Jack's hand. "Thank you for calling me. And I'm sorry. I truly am. We're going to fix this. I want KGU to be a place students are proud to attend. But I also want them to leave us with integrity and honor and good ethics."

"I'll know you'll do what's right," Jack said. "That's why I called you. I'd like you to sit in on the meeting we're about to have, but I'd like you to stay quiet until I hand over the floor to you. Once we close the case then you can do cleanup however you see fit."

"I appreciate it," Jim said.

Martinez, Wachowski, Riley, and Durrant preceded us into the conference room, and they stationed themselves around the perimeter of the room, joining Hops. Doug went in next with the sword, and then Jack and I stepped inside the crowded room. Jim came in last, and finally I saw something that looked like panic on Trish Johnson's face.

Jim took the seat directly across from Trish, and then he looked around at each of the individuals seated at the table.

"What's going on here?" David asked.

"That's going to be obvious enough pretty soon," Jack said. "But we're going to ask the questions from here on out. We're sorry to ruin everyone's Saturday, but the pesky details of murder keep getting in the way."

"This is stupid," Nikhil said. "None of us murdered Kevin. And if anyone did it was Dwight. Everyone saw him do it."

They all started talking at once and Dwight finally looked up from staring at his cuffs, the anger coming off him in palpable waves.

"Kevin was my friend," Dwight said, his voice

cracking. "My only friend. Because none of you are, that's for sure. You'll keep to the honor code as long as it keeps you looking spotless, but I guess the code only goes so far for me."

"Dwight," Trish said quietly, and Dwight's mouth clamped shut and he looked back at his cuffed hands. "Let's just let the sheriff say what he has to say. They haven't charged you with anything yet, and they would have if they had solid evidence."

Jack's smile was like a knife aimed at Trish. "Going to make a lateral transfer to the law school next?" he asked.

"Maybe," she said, and pushed back her chair. "My time here is up. If you're going to charge us, charge us. If not, we're all leaving."

"Sit down, Trish," Jim said, his voice ringing through the room. "Do it now. You will cooperate, and you will set a good example for these students or there will be consequences for everyone."

Trish and Jim stared at each other, and Trish finally scooted her chair back up to the table. "Fine," she said. "For now."

"Sorry, Jack," Jim said. "I won't interfere again."

"I appreciate you stepping in," Jack said. "Because I would have put them all in cuffs without blinking an eye. So you saved us the trouble."

I watched the students closely, and they started to fidget, the worry starting to seep in.

"Ahh," Jack said, looking around the circle of faces. "I wondered how long it would take you all to realize that she can't protect you forever. She's not even protecting you now. She doesn't have the same honor code she expects the rest of you to live by. You're all too smart to get caught up in this trap."

"What trap?" Savannah asked. "What's happening?"

"Lies, sex, cover-ups, manipulation..." Jack said. "Let's start four years ago. David, Kevin, Dwight, Chad, and Madison. You were all freshmen, just starting out, and Jaden was a sophomore. All of you had classes in the science, math, and engineering buildings. You had classes together. And you even had a common professor. Dr. Trish Johnson.

"She's dynamic and a great teacher, and her field of study would appeal to most of you, Madison excluded. But then she and David started sleeping together."

"Hey," David said, his fists balling on the table.

"Just pretend we all fall under the 'honor code,'" Jack said, making air quotes. "Because you can't tell me everyone at this table isn't aware of that. That's just one of the many secrets this groups holds. Just because something is protected under legal red tape and NDAs doesn't mean that no one knows. It just means they can't talk about it.

"But you two didn't just click in the bedroom. You clicked in the lab as well, and David having the brilliant mind he does was able to bring a fresh perspective to Trish's research. So much so that he was the one who discovered a brand-new hologram technology. That's pretty amazing, David. I'm sure the military is going to put you to good use if you ever graduate.

"Now Trish finds herself in a predicament," Jack continued. "She has knowledge of something both the scientific and academic world will revere. It's all about the science, right? I believe several of you have uttered that statement over the last couple of days. So Trish submits the new research to an academic journal and they publish it. The only problem is that Kevin knew it wasn't her work, and he reported the ethics violation. It cost you your reputation in the science world, your position, and the optical engineering program was shut down, but you didn't lose your job. You had tenure and they just moved you around on campus to another department since you were qualified.

"But I did a little research after you said you moved to the history department. At that time, the D&D club was student led. There were a handful of kids who got together and did live action role-play. And there were another handful who participated in the online quests and entered the tournaments individually. But you saw an opportunity to do two things if you made it an organized structure. The first was to keep your relationship with David going. There was no reason for you to lose everything. The second was that it kept you involved in the science. You could continue to use the resources in the labs and get information from the kids, and you could disguise it under teaching them something a little extra, even though the hologram department wasn't there. They still had the equipment, right? A lot of which is stored in your black box theater if I'm not mistaken."

"So what?" she asked. "Look what I've done with the organization. Do you know how much money this tournament would've brought into the university? We've been planning to host for more than a year. It's a huge coup for KGU."

"It's also a nice feather in your cap," Jack said. "It's pretty spectacular that one school would have five nationally ranked players in the top ten. Maybe that gives you a little bit of the credit you feel like you were cheated out of. That Kevin cheated you out of."

"I already told you he did what he thought was best at the time," she said. "It's the past."

"Because he didn't know any better, right?" Jack asked. "There were no Kings at that point. Kevin was just a nerdy kid who happened to be good at a game that paid for his tuition. But when you became the official sponsor and you saw the talent and potential of the Kings, these elite students who you could live through vicariously, the first thing you taught them was the honor code. Kevin just didn't know the honor code before, so you were able to explain it and forgive him. Once."

The kids weren't nearly as good at hiding their emotions as Trish, and several of them squirmed or looked down when Jack mentioned the honor code.

"Things were going good for you and the students," Jack continued. "Notoriety. The organization grew to a couple of hundred kids, and you made sure they all fit into a group somehow. But no one was like your Kings. They were the best. And they also brought extra funding for you and the group. And Kevin was the star.

"Dwight told me that no one was even close to him in points," Jack said. "Kevin was light-years ahead of everyone, including his teammates. No one could have caught up to him. And as we were studying the rules and regulations of the tournament, and also because we have something of an in with the High Council, we found out that Dr. Johnson gets an extra stipend for coaching the number one player.

"But things changed last spring when Kevin started tutoring Madison. That's when you worried your stipend might go away."

Trish made an effort to look bored, but her fists were clenched tight together.

"And in comes Chad," Jack said. "I wondered how you fit into the group, and then I remembered Dwight telling us that there were seven full-time Kings and two more that filled in when the story needed extra characters. You were one of the fill-ins, right?"

Chad nodded, but didn't say anything.

"I'm glad you're learning to tell the truth, because we found your prints all over Dwight's apartment. In fact, we found prints in Dwight's apartment for everyone at this table except for Dr. Coleman. You all knew each other. So it was no big deal for you to ask Kevin if he'd tutor your girl-friend in calculus," Jack told Chad. "But you have a reputation to uphold. Like everyone here, you like leading a double life, pretending you're someone you're not. Only for you it's your everyday persona you're pretending. You're just like everyone at this table. Only you don't want anyone to know you spend your weekends playing D&D or partici-pating in these tournaments.

"So much so that when we looked back at your quest records for the year, you didn't complete the task so you were automatically disqualified from this tournament. You couldn't hide since the tour-nament was on your own campus.

"But the other guys you hang out with aren't like you," Jack said, staring intently at Chad. "They wouldn't understand this group of misfits you iden-tify with more than your frat brothers. So why not plan a harmless prank on Kevin just to show them where your loyalties lie? It's not a big deal, right? Just good college fun? But you need Madison to make it more believable, so she sets out to seduce Kevin so he'll take her back to his room. And then we know what happened. Everyone on campus and most of the world knows what happened. You put Kevin's shame and misery out there for everyone to see. But it was just fun and games.

"But the problem was Kevin didn't just bounce back from a harmless prank. He went into a severe depression. He stopped going to classes, and went online. He became a hermit in his own dorm room, rarely leaving his bed or the room at all. Fortunately, he had a friend in Dwight. Someone to check on him and make sure he was okay. I guess none of you thought to check on Kevin," he said, looking around the table. "There's such a code of honor that you'd let him suffer in silence?"

Tears leaked from Savannah's eyes, and she wiped them, smearing dark eye makeup, and Jaden put his arm around her, glaring at Jack. I thought of all of them, Savannah might be the only one who was salvageable in the humanity department.

"Don't worry, because Dwight went every day and sat with Kevin while his world fell apart. But eventually he started to speak and eat and get out of bed. But he wasn't quite ready to get back into the world. Look at what being a King had brought him. He didn't want any part of that. As much as he loved Kaal Dracarian, he wasn't sure he could put himself on a stage where everyone would only be remembering the video instead of the champion he was.

"But that would be terrible news for the Kings." And then he looked at Trish. "Especially for you. Your stipend was based on points, and Kevin had a lot of points. You would have lost a considerable amount of money. And you couldn't let that happen."

Jack turned to Madison then, and she jumped lightly in her seat. "When did Dr. Johnson come to you and ask if you'd try to get Kevin to reconsider?"

"That's ridiculous," Trish said. "Don't answer that, Madison."

"Look at me," Jack said. "She has no power here over any of you. It's time to do the right thing for once. For all of you to do the right thing. Did she come to you about Kevin?"

Madison nodded shakily and then said, "Yes." She cleared her throat. "She asked me to persuade him to keep playing. She said whatever I had to do. It was important. She paid me a hundred dollars a week, and I didn't have anything else to do during the summer."

"So you told Chad what the arrangement was and y'all agreed to break up. You could convince Kevin that you had no idea what Chad had planned, and Chad agreed to back you up. You and Chad could date in secret while you kept Kevin involved in the Kings. You see, the issue isn't just that Trish would be losing her stipend. The issue was that Kevin knew the experiments that were being conducted in the black box theater. He knew the secrets of the Kings. Research, labs, academic study...all in the name of science. But if Kevin left the Kings he wouldn't be bound to the honor code. So it was paramount that he stayed in, whether he wanted to or not.

"But Kevin wasn't a fool. Not as much as the rest of you. He never believed Madison was sincere when she appealed to him to give her a second chance. He knew she was just as involved in his humiliation as Chad was. So why not take advantage of it? Just like Chad—just like all of you—the double life is intoxicating. You like the fantasy. Pretending to be something you're not. And when it doesn't turn out the way you planned, you can chalk it up to a failed experiment. Sometimes in science you have to keep experimenting until you get it right.

"But the tables were turned and you ended up being an experiment for Kevin," Jack said to Madison. "Things were going along just as you planned until sex came into the picture."

"What?" Chad yelled, kicking his chair away from Madison and staring at her with revulsion. "You were actually sleeping with him? You told me you were just playing the part. You told me you were just hanging out, but you had to make it look real."

Madison cringed and covered her face, her body shaking with sobs, and Martinez came and put his hand on Chad's shoulder, reminding him of where he was and warning him all at the same time. Chad kept his chair pushed away, but he went silent and his face went stony.

"But in the end Kevin played you for the fool," Jack said, his voice softer, gentler. "And he ruined the dreams you had for next year. Only when he showed you his revenge and broke things off with him, you already knew that your dreams were going to be different than you'd planned. You thought he was going to propose and you were going to tell him about the baby."

"The baby was Kevin's?" Chad croaked out, his face going red with anger. Martinez didn't move from directly behind him and he kept a firm hand on him. Chad looked like he could have killed Madison right at that moment.

"Yes," Madison said, her voice stronger than she looked. "The baby is Kevin's."

"You came to me and had sex with me so I would think it was mine," he said, the realization coming over him. "You bitch." And then Chad leaned over and put his face in his hands.

"Do you see how destructive this world y'all choose to live in is?" Jack asked all of them. "How living in a fantasy with the illusion that there are no rules or repercussions to your actions is a lie? You might be wondering how you got here or how things spiraled out of control. But did any of you stop to think about Kevin? You think he recovered so easily after what he went through? Do you really think Madison just strolled back into his life and he decided everything was okay again? You've lived in an environment of secrets and darkness for the last three years. How do you think that's going to impact you for the rest of your lives, especially now that you watched a friend die?"

"How...how does this help you find who killed Kevin?" Savannah asked.

"I think you already know the answer to that," Jack said. "Because some of the work you did behind closed doors was Dr. Johnson's and David's research on holograms. You all learned how to create them. You all helped with the research and advancing the technology. Maybe with all your minds put together Dr. Johnson could get her academic status back. But just like everything, Kevin was a cut above. He was smarter and more advanced, even outpacing the professor."

Jack took the sword from Doug and walked around the table, and the he flipped the switch and he watched the hologram roll across the blade like liquid fire and the electrical spark flash at the tip of the sword. Everyone at the table jumped, some pushing back and looking like they were going to run for the door.

"It's beautiful, isn't it?" Jack asked. "Our own experts say it's brilliantly done. This kind of work is exceptional. And you all know who it belongs to. It's like a calling card. Someone does something like this they might as well be signing their name to it. But just to be sure, we took the sword apart and dusted for fingerprints. You know whose fingerprints showed up?"

Everyone diverted their gaze, no one having the courage to look at the sword or Jack. "Dwight, you want to tell me whose fingerprints we found inside?"

Dwight lifted his head and looked at the sword in all its beauty, and then he looked at Jack. Dwight's face was ravaged by tears and grief. Of all of them, he'd been the only one who'd been a true friend to Kevin.

"It was Kevin's," Dwight finally said.

Jack nodded and turned off the sword, and then he laid it in the middle of the table. "That's right. It was Kevin's. As far as Kevin was concerned, there was no other way out. He was ridiculed and shamed in front of the world. A girl he tried to help turned on him. And then when he tried to escape to save his sanity, Dr. Johnson sent Madison back in to tie the noose a little tighter around his neck." Jack looked at Trish and his expression wasn't friendly. "Kevin couldn't escape the world you forced him into. He'd been trying to do the right thing since his freshman year, when he turned you in to the university. But you were always there, like the devil on his shoulder whispering in his ear. He finally had enough of it and decided it was much easier to become Kaal Dracarian than to stay Kevin Schwartzman. So he reeled Madison in and paid her back for her treachery. And then he decided if he was going to go viral it might as well be on stage in front of thousands of people. So while Dwight was out with the flu Kevin forged a sword that was worthy enough to die by. He calculated everything, from his armor placement to the material of the floor of the ring. He knew he would die in the fantasy he created, and then the hell he'd been living on earth would be over."

"I didn't know what he had planned," Dwight said, looking at Jack. "When I turned on the sword I knew it was him, just by looking at the hologram. No one could make anything as realistic as Kevin could. I thought he was doing me a favor. Helping me get extra points."

"I know," Jack said, and he nodded to Riley to undo the cuffs on Dwight's wrists. "The mistake was not telling me that you all recognized Kevin's work in that sword. You can all make choice from this point forward in how you treat people. Choose wisely. The irony of this whole thing is that Kevin's fingerprint was what told me the truth. So it looks like this time, it was all about the science."

Jack looked at Jim and said, "You're welcome to use the room for as long as you like. There are no arrests to be made, but I'm hoping you'll be able to inflict more pain than I can. The official cause of death will be amended to suicide."

"Thank you, Jack," Jim said, leaning back in his chair and looking shell-shocked. "I'm almost sorry you couldn't make an arrest. But there will definitely be consequences now that the whole story has come out. I appreciate you taking the time to try to teach what Dr. Johnson is incapable of."

Jack nodded and put his hand on Doug's shoulder as we all exited the conference room and left Coleman to deal with his staff and students.

I'd been watching Doug while Jack had been talking, and it was rare to see him somber and thoughtful for this long of a period of time. We were back at Jack's office when Doug asked, "How come you let me observe all that? There was no need for me to be there. I didn't do anything?"

"Sure you did," Jack said. "You helped work the

case. When you work for justice it's important to see the fruits of your labor."

"But no one was guilty," he said.

"You think not?" Jack asked, brow raised. "They're all going to have to live with their choices. With their own regrets and nightmares."

"Yeah, I guess," Doug said.

"I also wanted you to see that you're not like them," Jack said. "You could have been, but your Uncle Ben loved you enough to smack you down. When you have a brain like yours it's easy to think you'll always be able to outsmart everyone else. But that's not the case. It's not how smart we are or the work we do that counts in the long run. It's the people we care about."

Doug swiped his hair out of his eyes and said. "I guess I see your point. I don't want to be like them. None of them have a clue how terrible they were."

"You won't be," Jack said.

"How do you know?" Doug asked.

"Because you recognized how terrible they were, and now you'll remember them whenever you're faced with choices in your life."

"I think we've done all we can do with this case," I said, throwing my arm around Doug's shoulder and giving him a hug. "Why don't we go home?"

"I have a better idea," Doug said. "Why don't we stop at that diner across the square. I was doing a little research and apparently they have twelve different kinds of homemade pie."

I laughed and said, "You know you don't have to try all twelve in one sitting, right?"

"What's the fun in that?" he asked, slipping out of my grasp to go tell Martinez and Wachowski goodbye.

Jack put his arm around me and pulled me close. "Why don't we get some pie to go? We have a date in our bedroom the rest of the weekend. I'd hate for you to starve."

"Now you're talking my kind of romance," I said as we walked arm in arm out of the sheriff's office and into the crisp winter air.

EPILOGUE

"ARE YOU SURE ABOUT THIS?" CARVER ASKED, wheeling his wheelchair around the newly constructed half-court basketball court Jack had insisted on adding to our driveway.

It was early February, but it was one of the rare, teasing days where the sun shone brightly in a cloudless sky, so the cold didn't seem as harsh as the temperature gauge said. We'd been up since the early morning, making arrangements, ordering donuts, moving furniture so the painters could get in, ordering breakfast tacos, and unloading boxes of electronics and clothes.

"We're sure," Jack said, shooting a jump shot and swishing it in. When the ball came down he bounce-passed it to Carver.

"He'll cost you a fortune as long as you keep buying basketball courts and media rooms for him."

I was enjoying sitting on the bench with my

face raised to the sun, but I was listening intently to the conversation.

"We have a fortune to spend," I butted in. "Jack tells me that all the time. I've never seen this fortune, but apparently it's there."

Carver grinned and rolled his wheelchair closer to the basket so he could shoot from his wheelchair.

"Sounds like Michelle," he said. "She doesn't let me touch the money. I think she thinks I'll buy ridiculous things."

"That's probably a safe bet," Jack said, grabbing the rebound and doing a quick layup before tossing the ball back to Carver.

"Hey," Doug shouted from the second-story balcony. "They put this wood up on my wall and now they're painting it black."

"I thought you wanted black," I said.

Doug's face lit up. "I thought it was a mistake and you were going to have kittens or something. This is so awesome." He stepped back through the French doors and we could hear his whoop of joy through the glass.

"Well, you can always call me if things get crazy," Carver said. "I'm used to crazy around my house."

Jack laughed. "We'll be fine. I was a teenage boy once. I don't think they've changed all that much."

Carver held on to the ball and waited until Jack looked at him. "I want to say thank you for this. Truly. I mean it. It's just been Doug and my sister since he was a baby, and she's worked to give him everything she can. But she's never understood him. She loves him, but I think it frustrates her that she can't give him what he needs. And what he needs is a swift kick in the ass from time to time and constructive things to keep him busy."

"Which is why he'll be working mornings at the Donut Palace. Then he can come home and do his classes since they're all online. Doug's got a good head on his shoulders. He's going to be okay."

"And if you need a break you can always send him to our place for a night," Carver said.

"Convenient invitation since you live in DC," Jack said.

"You see, this is why Michelle controls the money. She got a real good deal on that remodeled Victorian on Hanover Street."

"Wait a second," I said, getting up from the bench. "Hanover Street in Bloody Mary?"

"That's the one," Carver said, grinning.

"You bought a house in Bloody Mary?" Jack asked, narrowing his eyes.

"Isn't that what I just said?" And then Carver looked at me. "He never listens. Now I know how Michelle feels."

I snorted out a laugh, joy filling me. It would be nice to have good friends that close by.

"What's going on?" Jack asked, not relenting. "What's wrong?"

"Nothing's wrong," Carver said, wheeling

himself backward and bounce-passing the ball to Jack.

"You're telling me you and Michelle and four kids have just decided to pick up and move to Bloody Mary for no reason?"

"Well, Doug is here now, and it'll be nice to be close. And you're here too. So that's like an added bonus. It's like having built-in babysitters. You've already got Doug, so what's four more from time to time."

"Substantial," Jack said, and then he said, "Ben, tell me what's going on."

Jack never used Carver's first name and it got both of our attention. But Carver shrugged and used his cheeky grin to try to make it seem like everything was fine.

"Things are getting interesting at work," Carver said. "I just felt like it was a good time to get out of the city."

"Are you safe?" Jack asked.

"For now. And that's all I can say."

Jack nodded and looked at me, and I could see the worry in his eyes for his friend. But there was no point in pressing further. Carver was as stubborn as a mule when he made his mind up about something.

Jack tossed the ball back to Carver. "You picked a good house."

"I'm glad you think so," Carver said. "Maybe you can convince Michelle. She'll be by later with the girls so we can go out to dinner."

"I'll put in a good word," Jack said, and then he caught the ball back from Carver and immediately passed it to me.

I held on to the ball and looked between Jack and Carver. There was something going on, but for now all we could do was wait for Carver to tell us what it was. Until then, there was a lot of life to live.

"Welcome to the neighborhood," I told Carver, passing him the ball. "I'll put in a good word for you with the sheriff. I hear he's a real pain in the a —" I didn't get to finish the sentence before Jack tackled me around the middle and had me over his shoulder in a fireman's carry.

"What was that?" he asked, smacking me on the behind.

I was laughing so hard tears streamed down my cheeks. "He's the greatest. And the sexiest. He's amazing," I said, gasping for breath.

Jack turned a quick circle that had my head spinning. "See, Carver," Jack said. "You've just got to know how to handle your woman."

"You're a fine example to us all," Carver said. "But your woman just stole your wallet out of your back pocket."

I went into a fit of giggles again and realized this was what I had been missing growing up. *This* was family. And these were the moments I would remember when I was old and gray. Because good always outshines the darkness.

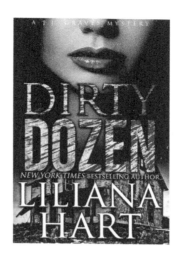

In the twelfth installment of the J.J. Graves mystery
series from New York Times Bestselling Author
Liliana Hart, winter has moved into Bloody Mary
with a vengeance. But so has a killer who's bringing
a modern flair in his imitation of Jack the Ripper.
It's up to J.J. and her husband, Sheriff Jack Lawson,
to hunt the hunter and bring justice to the victims.

Coming December 7, 2021! **Pre-Order Today**

ABOUT THE AUTHOR

Liliana Hart is a *New York Times, USA Today,* and Publisher's Weekly bestselling author of more than sixty titles. After starting her first novel her freshman year of college, she immediately became addicted to writing and knew she'd found what she was meant to do with her life. She has no idea why she majored in music.

Since publishing in June 2011, Liliana has sold more than eight-million books. All three of her series have made multiple appearances on the *New York Times* list.

Liliana can almost always be found at her computer writing, hauling five kids to various activities, or spending time with her husband. She calls Texas home.

If you enjoyed reading this, I would appreciate it if you would help others enjoy this book, too.

Recommend it. Please help other readers find this book by recommending it to friends, readers' groups and discussion boards.

Review it. Please tell other readers why you liked this book by reviewing.

Connect with me online:
www.lilianahart.com

facebook.com/LilianaHart
instagram.com/LilianaHart
bookbub.com/authors/liliana-hart

ALSO BY LILIANA HART

JJ Graves Mystery Series

Dirty Little Secrets

A Dirty Shame

Dirty Rotten Scoundrel

Down and Dirty

Dirty Deeds

Dirty Laundry

Dirty Money

A Dirty Job

Dirty Devil

Playing Dirty

Dirty Martini

Dirty Dozen

Addison Holmes Mystery Series

Whiskey Rebellion

Whiskey Sour

Whiskey For Breakfast

Whiskey, You're The Devil

Whiskey on the Rocks

Whiskey Tango Foxtrot

Whiskey and Gunpowder

Whiskey Lullaby

The Scarlet Chronicles

Bouncing Betty

Hand Grenade Helen

Front Line Francis

The Harley and Davidson Mystery Series

The Farmer's Slaughter

A Tisket a Casket

I Saw Mommy Killing Santa Claus

Get Your Murder Running

Deceased and Desist

Malice in Wonderland

Tequila Mockingbird

Gone With the Sin

Grime and Punishment

Blazing Rattles

A Salt and Battery

Curl Up and Dye

First Comes Death Then Comes Marriage

Box Set 1

Box Set 2

Box Set 3

The Gravediggers

The Darkest Corner

Gone to Dust

Say No More